"Brit, I recently

"An ugly divorce.

"And as a result—

"You're steering clear of relationships. I get it. So let's agree not to have one."

Looked like she was rejecting him before he even asked. Alrighty, then. "I wasn't planning on it."

"Neither am I. Tonight will be one and done."

His body jerked as if she'd smacked him upside the head. "*What?*"

"Unless we're not on the same page. In that case, I've just made a huge fool of myself."

He sucked in a breath and rushed to erase that misperception. "Oh, we're on the same page. But...you'd be okay with that?"

"More than okay. This whole setup is turning me on — the drinks, my birthday, riding in your fabulous truck, that song, the way you look in a hat, the—"

"My hat? Really?" Rance also had a hat and a badass truck, but she'd turned him down.

"Well, *duh*. You're dynamite without it, but once you put on that Stetson, you become the whole package." She started to giggle. "Whoops. Freudian slip."

BLOWING THE COWBOY'S MIND

ROWDY RANCH

Vicki Lewis Thompson

Ocean Dance Press

BLOWING THE COWBOY'S MIND
© 2024 Vicki Lewis Thompson

ISBN: 978-1-63803-921-1

Ocean Dance Press LLC
PO Box 69901
Oro Valley, AZ 85737

This is a work of fiction. Any resemblance to actual persons, living or dead, business establishments, events, or locales is entirely coincidental.

Visit the author's website at
VickiLewisThompson.com

_1_

"Okay, Armstrong, the crowd's thinning out, so I'll be shoving off. You're in charge."

Trent added a fourth mug of cider to the tray sitting on the Fluffy Buffalo's antique bar and Cecily whisked it away. "Think I can handle it, McLintock?" He looked across the bar at Rance, who had his shearling jacket hooked over his shoulder.

"Sadly, I do." Rance chuckled. "I might've made a mistake asking Clint to hire you. You're making me look bad."

"I could always quit." Although he'd enjoyed being a part-timer at the Buffalo the past couple of months. Tending bar while being serenaded by a crackerjack country band was a nice break from staring at a computer screen all day.

"Nah, you can't quit." Rance nudged back his Stetson. "I'm still hoping this gig will inspire you to get back in the game."

No, and hell no. But he wouldn't say that to Rance, whose heart was in the right place. Grabbing a bar rag, he wiped a few drops of cider from the polished surface. Then he glanced up. "Guess I need more time."

"Or maybe you need to take that leap of faith. When you fall off the horse—"

"Correction. I was bucked off."

"I get that, but—"

"Hey, Trent, the birthday celebration ladies want another round of red, white and blues," Cecily called out as she hurried toward the bar. She slid her empty tray in Trent's direction. "Ella's is virgin, don't forget."

"No, ma'am, I won't."

"I have to keep reminding myself since she's not showing yet."

"Same here." Ella and Marsh's baby announcement in February had brought great joy to Rowdy Ranch in general and Desiree McLintock in particular.

Pulling out three tall glasses, he started concocting the layered drinks as the band launched into the Garth Brooks classic *Friends in Low Places*.

Midway through the process he gave Rance a quick look. "I thought you were heading out."

"I was." He stared at his phone. "And I will. By the way, Brit's drinks are free."

"They are?"

"It's our birthday policy. Hers is technically tomorrow, but coming into the Buffalo the night before is now a tradition for her, Faye and Ella. That's when they collect their freebies."

"I'll fix the tab. Thanks for the heads-up."

"Hard to believe Brit's turning thirty-one. I still think of her as Casey Cougar, revving up the crowd at the games."

"The mascot?"

"All four years. When I came in as a freshman, she was the most popular person in school. Folks still say she was the best Casey Cougar WTHS ever had."

"That's impressive." He took a quick peek at the slim, dark-haired woman with Ella and her sister Faye. Since he lived out at Rowdy Ranch, he was well acquainted with those two, who'd each married a McLintock. He'd never met Brit, though.

She had great hair, lustrous and wavy, long enough to brush her shoulders during her animated conversation with her buddies. She was petite, so no wonder she was flushed after a couple of the potent red, white and blues. Clearly a fun-loving lady, though. "I always thought being a school mascot would be a tough job."

"I'm sure it is, but she made it look easy."

"Sounds like somebody's got a crush."

"Nope. She's too high-energy for me."

"Let me guess. She turned you down."

Rance sighed. "She did, but it was for the best. I recently had an epiphany."

"Was that an out-patient procedure or did you have to stay overnight?"

"Very funny."

"I thought so." He got a kick out of Rance's rich vocabulary. The guy loved throwing out words that most people never used.

"I need somebody who'll calm me down, not ramp me up. A woman who'll keep me from going off the rails. In other words, the female equivalent of my brother Lucky."

"Interesting insight." He stuck a cherry on top of Ella's virgin drink to differentiate it from the other two. "These are good to go, Cecily."

Rance whistled softly and tapped his phone. "Damn, Armstrong. Eight minutes, twelve seconds for three layered drinks, including one virgin. While carrying on a conversation. That's intimidating."

"You timed me?"

"I was curious. Would've taken me closer to ten. You have skills, my friend."

"Thanks."

"You know, Brit's all wrong for me, but she might be just the ticket for—"

"Stop right there. I know you mean well, but I—"

"You've got the yips."

That made him smile. "I suppose I do. Also, I see no point in dating when I'll never get married again."

"You say that now, but—"

"I'm telling you, I'm done with that institution. It's not for me."

"All right, but what about sex?"

"That's a problem. But I'm not into meaningless hookups, either."

Rance grinned. "Which puts you between a rock and a hard—"

"Never mind."

"Sorry. I shouldn't tease you about it. She must have done a number on you."

"Yeah." He met Rance's sympathetic gaze. "She did."

"I'd rather chew her out in person, but New Jersey's a bit of a hike. Hey, I could call her, though. Like right now. Given the time difference, I'd wake her up. That would be fun."

"The eleven-year-old in me loves that idea."

"Okay, let's prank her." Rance lifted his phone, his expression eager. "What's her—"

"I'm not giving it to you. Harassing her in the middle of the night is juvenile."

"What if I don't harass her? What if I thank her for giving you a better life? I'll tell her you've got rock-hard abs, a fire-breathing horse and a badass truck. Then I'll mention that the ladies are flocking—"

"You're not calling her."

"Aw, come on. Let me plant the bitter seeds of regret in her heart."

He snorted. "Fertilized with a bunch of BS?"

"It's all true. Well, except the part about the ladies, who actually would come flocking if you'd stop putting up *No Trespassing* signs. I've seen women giving you the eye. Brit was doing it a little while ago, but you were oblivious."

"Was she?" His pulse rate picked up. Seems he couldn't stop his natural reaction to attention from a pretty woman.

"Definitely. Pay attention and you'll see I'm right."

"Odds are she's looking for something permanent."

"Possibly. As far as I know, she's never even been engaged, but now that all her friends are coupling up...peer pressure and all that." Rance pushed away from the bar. "Alrighty, I'm outta here. Clint's scheduled us to work together on Tuesday night. You good with that?"

"Wouldn't miss it."

"Excellent." He touched the brim of his hat and started down the hall toward the back door. "We make a good team," he hollered over his shoulder.

"We do," Trent called back. They got along well, probably because he was quiet and thoughtful, a lot like Rance's brother Lucky.

He'd played that role with Cheryl, too, until she'd decided to play with someone else. Taking a deep breath, he derailed that train of thought by focusing on his present environment, which had a lot going for it.

The couples on the floor knew their way around a two-step, and the talented lead guitarist in the band had given them just the tune they needed to show it off.

The remaining customers looked happy to be here and he couldn't blame them. The Buffalo had more character and charm than any bar he'd ever walked into.

As he scanned the room, he skipped quickly past Brit, but brief eye contact told him Rance was right. She was watching him. Or maybe it was her position at the table creating that impression.

He glanced at her again. Yeah, she was definitely looking at him. When he met her gaze, a smile lit up her face.

It triggered one of his own. Couldn't help himself. He quickly looked away. She was likely guilty of flirting while tipsy. If he kept his focus elsewhere for the rest of the evening, he'd nip that in the bud.

2

"He just smiled at me." Brit kept her gaze on Trent in case he might look her way again.

Ella laughed. "Congratulations. Maybe you'll be the one to thaw his frozen heart."

"He's pretty hot. I'd be tempted to try if I hadn't been burned by Jeff."

"He might be recently divorced like Jeff was, but that's the only thing they have in common," Faye said. "Jeff played the poor-me game so you'd knock yourself out consoling him. Trent's working through this on his own. I admire that."

"I admire his butt. Whoops, did I say that out loud?" Brit giggled.

Ella peered at her. "How can you even see his butt? Have these red, white and blues given you X-ray vision?"

"I wish, but evidently they've only removed my filter."

"So you're imagining he has a cute butt."

"Don't have to. About an hour ago he took a break and I watched him walk down the hall toward the restrooms. And walk back. Now I can imagine him naked."

"Whoa." Faye's eyes widened. "You've really been paying attention."

"I'm storing up images and hoping they'll appear in my dreams tonight. You two don't need that kind of stimulating visual anymore now that you have permanent bed partners, but I—"

"Brittany Jane Powers." Ella leaned toward her, her blue gaze intent. "Find. A. Husband. ASAP."

"It's not that easy! Wagon Train's a small town and most of the eligible guys are either married or not my type."

"Because you've been loafing on the lead," Faye said. "You say you want marriage and kids, but have you seriously looked for a baby-daddy?"

"Sort of. I'm picky."

Ella rolled her eyes. "Tell me something I don't know."

"Forever is a long damn time, El. I haven't met anyone I've looked at and said oh, yeah, I want to see that face across the breakfast table for the rest of my life."

"What about him?" Faye tipped her head toward the bar. "He's clearly your type, and I'm telling you, he's not Jeff, Part Two."

"You said it's only been six months since his divorce. I didn't want to believe that rule about not dating for a year but after Jeff I absolutely do."

"That's the common wisdom," Faye said, "but Trent strikes me as someone who doesn't fit that rule, someone who deserves a second chance. Back me up, here, El. I know you really like Trent."

"I do. I figured I would since he's Dallas's brother and I like him a lot."

"That's right. Trent was Dallas's best man at the wedding."

Faye grinned. "Were you mentally undressing him that day, too?"

"I could barely see him. That's what I get for being short. I was stuck behind three tall people who blocked my view."

"How about at the reception?"

"Again, too many people and I wasn't exactly trying to locate him. Has he always had those muscles?"

"No," Ella said. "He's bulked up a lot since February. I think it's from working in the barn so much. He's really taken to ranch life, even has a horse, now."

"And a gorgeous blue truck," Faye added.

"Where'd he get the money for that? Bartending doesn't—"

"He's a self-employed marketing consultant," Ella said. "Rance convinced him to take a parttime bartending job in hopes it would bring him out of his shell. Turns out he enjoys it."

"That's obvious. He's good at it, too. He put these layered drinks together like a pro."

"And they're delicious." Ella took another sip of hers. "Dallas said he worked his way through college tending bar and then kept doing it for fun even after he created his marketing business. That's how he met his ex."

"And what's the story on her?" Not that she should be asking, but after all this discussion, she couldn't help being curious.

Ella's eyes narrowed. "Dallas describes her as a trophy hunter. Once she'd bagged Trent, she went looking for a side hustle."

"I shouldn't have asked." Brit sighed. "Now I feel sorry for him."

"The point is he doesn't feel sorry for himself." Ella looked over at Faye. "I think you nailed it when you said he was someone who deserves a second chance."

"Yep." Faye turned to her. "You may not be able to see from this distance, but he has beautiful brown eyes."

"I noticed." She'd spent the evening cataloging his features — his chiseled jaw, his sensuously full lips, his dark lashes, his beautiful teeth. She had a thing about teeth after cleaning them five days a week.

"Think you'd want to see that face across the breakfast table for the rest of your life?"

The concept created a flutter in her stomach. "Maybe." She took another swallow of her drink. "But I'm sure that's the booze talking."

3

At the stroke of midnight, the band closed up shop. A scattering of customers, including Brit, Ella and Faye, polished off their drinks and left. Cecily offered to help put up the chairs and sweep the floor, but Trent told her he'd handle it.

Setting the Buffalo to rights after a busy Saturday night was immensely satisfying. Although he'd enjoyed working in a couple of different bars in Trenton, he loved spending time in this one.

After locking the front door, he flipped off the switch that activated the wooden moose's greeting and turned on the sound system. He let shuffle play choose the songs as he upended the chairs onto the tables in preparation for sweeping.

Wouldn't you know, Brit had left her small denim purse hanging on the back of hers. He wasn't surprised, considering the way she and Faye had been giggling as Ella had shepherded them out the door.

He set it on the bar and keys jingled inside. She'd better have an alternative to getting into her house. He worried about that for a couple of seconds, then dismissed it. Ella would handle any issues.

Grabbing a push broom, he swept dirt and random bits of trash into a pile as Keith Urban sang *Somebody Like You*. Catchy tune, even if the words laid out a fantasy he didn't believe in anymore.

He missed being in love, missed the euphoria that had gripped him when he'd been convinced he would spend a lifetime with the woman of his dreams.

Blissful ignorance. Lovely while it lasted, hell when it ended. Never again would he allow himself to....

A persistent tapping broke into his thoughts and he glanced toward the front door. The etched oval of glass revealed a blurry image. Someone was outside. Could be Brit coming back for her purse.

Leaning the broom against the nearest table, he moved quickly past the now-silent buffalo and opened the door.

"Oh, thank goodness." Coatless, she hugged herself against the chill of a May evening. "I was afraid you couldn't hear me with the music playing. I think I left my purse."

"You did." He stepped away and ushered her in.

"Oh, thank God it's here and not in Ella's truck."

"She's not out there?" He checked the empty street.

"She's on the way back to Rowdy Ranch."

"I don't get it. Why would she just leave you—"

"She took me home. But Faye was feeling woozy so I hopped out and told Ella to take off. I didn't realize I didn't have my purse until I was standing on my front porch and she was long gone. I'd either left it in her truck or here. I'm glad it was here." She hurried over to the bar. "Now I can get into my house."

"You walked?"

"It's only a few blocks and the fresh air helped sober me up. Anyway, thanks for letting me in." She headed for the door.

"Give me a few minutes to finish up and I'll drive you home."

She turned back. "Aww, that's sweet of you to offer, but it's not necessary."

"It may not be necessary, but it's the right thing to do."

"Why?"

"Because... you're a customer."

Amusement sparkled in her blue eyes. "Do you usually give customers a ride home?"

"No, but it's late, and you—"

"I'm not drunk, if that's what you're worried about. At least I'm not as drunk as I was when I left here. And Wagon Train's streets are completely safe. I'll be fine."

She was right, of course, but letting her walk back alone violated his deeply ingrained sense of chivalry. "Just have a seat at the bar. Please. I won't be long."

"I don't want you going to the trouble. I— whoops, that's my phone." She pulled it out of her purse as it played the *Happy Birthday* song, which made for an interesting contrast to Johnny Cash's *Ring of Fire*. She tapped the screen and tucked the phone back in her purse.

"You're not answering? At this hour it could be impor—"

"It wasn't a call. It's my alarm. I set it to play *Happy Birthday* at 1:12 am, the time I was born." She flashed him a radiant smile. "I'm officially thirty-one."

He knew people who complained about getting older after they passed thirty. She clearly wasn't one of them. "Then let me be the first to wish you happy birthday."

"Thanks."

"And you shouldn't have to walk home by yourself now that your birthday is officially here. That's just wrong."

She studied him for a moment, her mouth tilted in a smile. "You make a valid point. I accept your kind offer."

"Good." What do you know. He'd finally invited a woman to occupy the passenger seat of his truck. Rance was bound to tease him about it. Well, unless he failed to mention this incident. Maybe he'd keep it to himself.

4

Brit hopped up on a bar stool and resisted the urge to twirl around. It used to be one of her favorite things when she was a kid, and she had just enough of a buzz left to feel like acting silly.

But Trent Armstrong didn't strike her as a guy who was into silly. She wasn't even convinced he liked her, although he'd given her a dazzling smile tonight that had curled her toes. Then he'd ignored her.

She'd been miffed about that for a while, and then she'd concluded it was for the best, with him being divorced and all.

Guaranteed he had issues. She had to watch out for her rescue tendencies, which had kicked in big time with Jeff. Big mistake. She was a dental hygienist, not a therapist. She'd be wise to steer clear of Trent Armstrong.

But damn, he was gorgeous. His New Jersey accent intrigued her, too. Since he'd insisted on seeing her safely home tonight, would it be so bad to invite him in for a nightcap?

Yes, it would. She'd been fantasizing about him all evening, and she was still slightly toasted, which tended to make her amorous.

She would *not* take his head-in-the-sand attitude toward dating as a challenge. She would curb the temptation to lure him out of his self-imposed exile.

That said, watching him wield a dustpan and broom, she developed a mild case of lust. Tight buns and broad shoulders had that effect on her, especially when she'd spent the evening drinking and she'd been celibate for several months.

The tunes on the sound system added fuel to the fire. When Luke Combs sang *The Kind of Love We Make,* she had no trouble picturing Trent stretched out on her queen-sized bed.

But despite the ringing endorsement from Ella and Faye, she didn't consider him marriage material. Ella and Faye were absolutely right. If she wanted children, she'd better get serious about finding a husband.

"Got big plans for tomorrow?"

"You mean today?"

He kept sweeping. "Okay, then, later today."

"Going up to Glacier National Park. It's a family tradition for my birthday."

"Sounds great. Should be beautiful."

"It always is."

"I'll bet. Alrighty, I'm done." Trent paused to glance at her. "I need to put everything in the kitchen, shut off the lights and fetch my jacket and hat. We'll be going out the back door, so if you want to come with me, I'll—"

"Can I just wait here?" Once he was out of sight, she'd give the stool a whirl.

"Sure." Carrying the broom and dustpan, he went behind the bar and cut off the music.

The minute he stepped into the kitchen, she spun around. When it slowed, she did it again, because with no one sitting on either side, she could really get it going.

Then Trent must have thrown the main switch, because everything went out except the security lights. How deliciously spooky. So what if he came back and found her acting like a kid? She spun faster, pushing hard against the bar as the shadows danced and blurred.

"Having fun?"

"Yep!" She grabbed the bar and stopped herself. "But now I'm dizzy. Give me a moment."

"Take your time." He sounded amused.

Maybe he wasn't as straightlaced as she'd thought. "I couldn't get away with that during business hours."

"Oh, you could, but I'd have to clear the stools on either side."

Carrying on a conversation in semi-darkness automatically made it more intimate. He'd also put on his Stetson, adding a heavy dose of cowboy sex appeal. "Would you clear the other two stools?"

"For the birthday girl? Of course."

Birthday girl. It wasn't an endearment, but close. They should probably get out of here. Sliding off the stool, she picked up her purse. "I'm ready."

"Put this on. It's cold out there." He held his jacket so all she had to do was turn and slide her arms in.

She opened her mouth to protest. Wearing his jacket would coax her further down the path of an attraction she should avoid.

"Take it. I got warmed up while I was sweeping so I don't need this. Besides, it's your birthday."

So it was, and rejecting his gallant gesture wasn't very polite. "Okay. That's sweet of you." Setting down her purse she turned and slid her arms into the soft fabric of his suede jacket.

He settled it on her shoulders. "Let me fix the sleeves." Moving in front of her, he expertly rolled them up so they didn't hang past her fingertips.

His light touch made her tingly. "Thanks." She retrieved her purse. "You do that well. Do you often loan out your jacket to short people?"

"Not really. When my sisters were little they'd wear my dad's old shirts when they were doing art projects. I'd help with the sleeves."

What an endearing tidbit. He'd probably picked up the *birthday girl* phrase from having two sisters.

"And we're off." He pulled his keys from his pocket and started toward the back of the building.

Hugging his warm jacket close, she fell into step beside him. "I'm guessing birthdays are a big deal in your family."

"They are. My folks took great pains to make them special. They still try to, although it's not so easy now that Dallas and I are out here."

"When's yours?"

"July 14th. They were going to celebrate it while they're out here for the wedding, but my sister Lani's is August 4th, so instead everybody's coming out then and we'll combine mine with hers." He opened the back door.

She was instantly grateful for the loan of his jacket as she stepped into the alley behind the building. The temperature had dropped significantly. "I'm so looking forward to this wedding. I still can't believe Desiree's getting married."

"I'm not positive she believes it, either. Andy does, though. He'll make sure it happens." Opening the passenger door, he helped her into the truck.

She was perfectly capable of getting in by herself, despite being barely five-two. But he accomplished the move before she could reach for the grab handle to haul herself up. And doggone it, she'd enjoyed being helped in.

Closing the door, he rounded the hood and climbed into the driver's seat. "Buckled up?" He took off his hat and laid it on the dash.

"Working on it." Even though the coat sleeves were rolled back, they kept getting in her way.

"I'll do it." He leaned close and took hold of the strap, bringing with him a heady combination of pine scented cologne and something more subtle that sent a rush of awareness through her body.

Her breath caught. If he turned his head, he'd be in range to kiss her.

Instead he concentrated on his task, shoved the tongue into the buckle and settled back into his seat.

"Thanks." Was she imagining that he was breathing differently as he fastened his own seatbelt? No, she wasn't.

"You're welcome." He switched on the engine and the radio played the last chords of a Shania Twain song. The full-bodied tones ended abruptly as he pushed a button on the dash.

"Could we leave it on? That sound quality is amazing."

"Um, sure." He tapped it again and Jason Aldean's *Burnin' It Down* poured from the truck's top-of-the-line speakers.

Oh, boy. She was in trouble. Couldn't get much more seductive than a handsome, wounded cowboy driving a brand-new truck with a primo sound system playing a song about sex. When the engine rumbled to life, the vibrations put her lady parts on high alert.

"I'll need directions." The huskiness in his voice gave him away. Whether he wanted to or not, he was having the same thoughts she was.

"Northeast corner of Maple and Stone." She could either ignore the evidence or act on it.

Her better self urged her to ignore the tension building between them as the powerful truck rolled down the asphalt. But her better self didn't stand a chance against Jason Aldean's voice coaxing her to go for it.

And after all, it was her birthday.

5

Only hours ago Trent had told Rance that he wasn't into meaningless hookups. Now that was exactly what he wanted. But he couldn't speak for Brit.

She was attracted to him. He got that loud and clear. Her breathing was as wonky as his and the sweet aroma of aroused woman teased him unmercifully. But like he'd also told Rance, she was probably looking for something permanent.

They needed to talk about it before they reached the northeast corner of Maple and Stone, and that location was coming up fast. He cleared his throat, had to speak up over the arousing music. "Brit, I recently went through—"

"An ugly divorce. Ella told me."

"And as a result—"

"You're steering clear of relationships. I get it. So let's agree not to have one."

Looked like she was rejecting him before he even asked. Alrighty, then. "I wasn't planning on it."

"Neither am I. Tonight will be one and done."

His body jerked as if she'd smacked him upside the head. "*What*?"

"Unless we're not on the same page. In that case, I've just made a huge fool of myself."

He sucked in a breath and rushed to erase that misperception. "Oh, we're on the same page. But...you'd be okay with that?"

"More than okay. This whole setup is turning me on — the drinks, my birthday, riding in your fabulous truck, that song, the way you look in a hat, the—"

"My hat? Really?" Rance also had a hat and a badass truck, but she'd turned him down.

"Well, *duh*. You're dynamite without it, but once you put on that Stetson, you become the whole package." She started to giggle. "Whoops. Freudian slip."

"Uh-huh." So what did he have that Rance didn't? Timing. He'd been the guy closing the bar on the eve of her birthday. He'd keep that in mind before he got all full of himself because she'd chosen him.

He'd thank his lucky stars for this opportunity. She was extremely likeable on top of being sexy as hell. He wasn't sure why she was so sexy. She had a gymnast's build, more lithe than curvy. Not his type at all.

Yet he couldn't wait to get his hands on her. The prospect of that sent an urgent message to his groin and made driving a torture he longed to end ASAP.

He pulled up in front of a tidy bungalow and glanced at her. "We're here."

"Then come on in, cowboy." Her voice had a breathy quality.

He shut off the engine and the music with it. Then he glanced at her. "Just to be clear, I don't normally—"

"Neither do I. I barely know you."

"Then maybe we shouldn't—"

"Listen, you're just looking for sex. Am I right?"

His face heated. "That sounds terrible."

"Not to me. All I want is some hot birthday action. Does that sound terrible?"

"Nope." It sounded freaking amazing.

"I have no intention of starting something with you."

That stung a little. "Why not?"

"You aren't ready."

That stung a little more. "I appreciate your honesty."

"I figured you'd be relieved to hear that. I'm hoping to find Mr. Right, but in the meantime…."

"You feel like celebrating your birthday?"

"Yes, I do."

"Then we'll do that." Unsnapping his seatbelt, he reached for the door handle when a blindingly obvious hurdle popped into his head. He sank back in defeat. "We can't. I don't have any—"

"I do."

He looked over at her, his hopes rising along with his eager cock. But had she checked the date on those convenient little items?

She met his gaze. "They haven't expired."

"Ah."

"Are we on?"

He swallowed. "Yes, ma'am." He broke eye contact and clutched the steering wheel as a wave of lust left him shaking. Then he reached for the door handle again. "Stay there. I'll—"

"I could use help with my seatbelt."

Leaning over the console, he released the buckle. And then he was kissing her. Maybe he started it. Maybe she did. Didn't matter. He had possession of her delicious mouth and his brain checked out.

She tasted citrus flavored with a no-holds-barred sensuality that left him gasping. He pulled back only to capture her lips again, thrusting his tongue deep. She tunneled her fingers through his hair and held him close as she opened to him with a desperate moan.

He lost track of where they were, of what made sense. He reached under the coat he'd loaned her and slipped his hand inside her shirt, craving the sensation of warm, smooth skin, the swell of her breasts under her silky bra, the—

She tightened her grip on his head and drew back, her breath coming fast. "We should…go in."

They should. Making out in his truck wouldn't achieve what they both needed. He gulped for air. "I…didn't mean to kiss you." His voice sounded like ice in a blender.

"You didn't. I kissed you."

"Oh."

"Couldn't help it. But if we're going to—"

"Understood." He eased away, reluctantly sliding his hand free. "I'll help you out." Snatching up his hat from the dash, he exited the truck, groaning as his jeans pinched him hard.

Taking his hat was stupid. It was the middle of the night, for God's sake. But his ego demanded that he wear it since the Stetson turned her on. He tugged on the brim.

She'd made it clear he wasn't worthy of more than a one-night stand, but in this moment, she couldn't resist him. He should be thrilled she didn't want to get involved. He *was* thrilled. That made tonight perfect.

He opened her door and she flashed him a grin.

"You put on your hat."

"When something works, might as well go with it." Scooping her out of the truck, he put her down and flung the door shut. "No more kissing until we're inside."

"Don't worry. I won't attack you until we're within reach of those little raincoats." She sashayed down the cement walkway. "Come with me, cowboy."

"I fully intend to." He lengthened his stride and ignored the pain in his privates.

"Sexy talk. I like it."

She was setting the tone. He'd make sure to stay in his role as temporary guy, the one who was available when she needed to scratch an itch.

And wasn't that how he saw her? He wasn't looking for dreamy-eyed gazes and heartfelt sighs. He'd stumbled into a situation where the birthday girl needed a man for the night. He'd be a fool to pass that up.

Cold air cut through his cotton shirt. Good thing he'd given her his jacket. It engulfed her small frame, which plucked at his heartstrings. He put a lid on that tender emotion.

He'd best lock down all his emotions. Tonight's episode was restricted to physical pleasure. He'd never had that kind of sex, but it was too late to question the premise.

The porch light was on but the inside of the one-story house was dark. He climbed the steps to the porch, his body throbbing as he waited for her to unlock the door.

She shoved it open. "Follow me." Without turning on a light, she took off.

He walked in and closed the door behind him. He couldn't see very well but he didn't have to. Her ragged breathing pinpointed her whereabouts, along with the rapid click of her bootheels on the wood floor.

Even without those clues, he could have found her through scent alone. Her body called to him and he was more than ready to answer.

He caught movement, something flung through the air that landed with a plop. Likely his jacket.

"You take off your clothes and I'll take off mine."

He smiled at her rapid-fire command. "Yes, ma'am." He started on the button on his cuff as he followed her into the hallway. Anticipation made him clumsy and he let out a soft swearword.

"You okay?"

"Just a case of fumble fingers."

She responded with a breathless laugh. "Me, too."

After undoing enough buttons that allowed him to pull his shirt over his head, he yanked it off. "Should I just drop stuff?"

"I did."

His boot landed on something that wasn't floor. "And I stepped on it."

"Never mind. Just my shirt. We're here. Doorway's on your right."

He didn't need directions. He swore he could feel the heat coming off her as he walked in. Through a window on the far side of the room, the glittering night sky gave him enough light to make out four tall bedposts. He hung his hat on the closest one.

Toeing off his boots, he stripped down, kicking his jeans and briefs away, tugging off his socks. Her slender silhouette taunted him as she tossed back the covers. He wanted to see her, but this was her show and clearly she preferred the dark.

Her footsteps whispered over the wood floor as she rounded the bed to the far side. "Go ahead and get in. I'll be with you in a second."

The scrape of a wooden drawer told him she was fetching the condoms. Then came the distinctive rip of a foil wrapper. Maybe they'd ditch foreplay and head straight for the main event.

He slid onto the sheets and lay on his back, gasping as his hot skin came in contact with cool cotton. His cock ached as if someone had clamped it in a vise and his heart pounded like it would explode any second.

The mattress barely moved as she climbed in and crawled toward him. "I have something for you." She straddled him, her smooth calves pressing against his thighs.

The breath left his lungs. "I hope it's—"

"This?" She rolled on the condom.

"Yep." He clenched his jaw and his fists. He was so close. So damn close.

Rising over him, she settled the tip of his cock at the entrance to paradise.

He held very still and used every ounce of control he possessed to keep from coming.

"There." She flattened her palms on his heaving chest and leaned down, her mouth nearly touching his. "I've got you where I want you."

"Ditto, sweet lady." He grasped her hips and lifted his, deepening the connection.

Her breath caught. Then with a cry of surrender, she took all of him, gasping and quivering in the grip of her climax.

Sheer stubbornness kept him from coming with her. She wanted a stud for her birthday and he would by God fulfill that request.

6

When Brit's world stopped spinning, she checked on how Trent was doing. She couldn't see his face very well, but he looked like he was smiling. "You didn't come."

"No, ma'am. I did not."

Definitely smiling. She heard it in his voice, along with a cockiness that revved her engines. "I thought for sure you would."

"I held off." He slid his hands under her backside and squeezed gently. "I'm thinking you might need another one."

"I just might." Her palms registered his rapid heartbeat. He wasn't as calm as he sounded.

Clearly he'd worked on his staying power, which indicated he cared about pleasing his partner. Good sign. She'd take him up on his offer of a second helping, but this time she'd coax him to join her. Mutual orgasms were more fun.

She began to slowly pump her hips. "How's that?"

He swallowed. "Very nice."

"Just nice?"

"Better than nice."

"I should hope so." The first round had ended so soon that his endowments hadn't truly registered.

Now that she was taking the measure of the man, so to speak, *nice* didn't begin to cover what he brought to the party. Judging from how fast he was breathing, he liked how she was treating his bad boy.

The intense friction worked so well she couldn't help speeding up the action. Oh, yeah. Hell, yeah.

The rasp of his breathing quickened and his fingers dug into her tush with an urgency that had been missing earlier.

She took it up another notch. "Gonna come this time?"

"Could be." His voice was thick with tension.

"Go for it." The guy had denied himself female companionship for months. He needed this as much as she did. She put on the afterburners. Ah, yes... there, right *there.*

At the moment of her release, he surged upward, meeting her downward thrust with a deep-throated growl. His big body went rigid and then shuddered as he came with a gratifyingly loud yell. Mission accomplished.

As her breathing slowed, she leaned down and feathered a kiss over his lips. "Better, now?"

"Much." Stroking her back, he let out a long, contented sigh. "Hope I didn't wake your neighbors."

"No worries. I have solid walls and double-paned windows. I'm glad you let go."

"Like I had a choice. You have moves, lady."

"I try." Giving him one more quick kiss, she slowly eased away from him and stretched out on her back. "That felt great."

"Now comes the challenging part." He sat up. "Where's—"

"The door's about six steps away."

"I see it. But I could use some more light."

"You bet." Rolling to her side, she reached for the lamp on the nightstand and switched it on.

"Thanks."

"Welcome." She turned back and was treated to a stunning view of broad shoulders, tight buns and muscled thighs as he headed toward the bathroom. Her fantasy had come to life and it was so much better than what she'd created in her head.

Making love in the dark had been her choice, but her first glimpse of Trent Armstrong naked showed her the error of her ways. "Mind if I leave the light on?"

"I wish you would." He flipped the wall switch in the bathroom. "I'm a visual guy."

"Most men are. But since we don't really know each other, I thought having sex in the dark would keep it from being awkward."

He ran water in the sink. "Did you feel awkward?"

She laughed. "Can't say I did. How about you?"

"I didn't have time to feel awkward. I was too busy making sure I didn't come in the first ten seconds."

"That was generous of you, by the way."

"I have my standards." He turned off the water. "Is it okay if I use one of your towels?"

"Of course." She propped a couple of pillows against the headboard and leaned against them. "Use anything you want. In fact, I'm shirking my hostess duties. Can I get you something?"

He chuckled. "I think you just did."

"Seriously." She sat up, swung her legs over the edge of the bed and stood. "I have beer, wine, snacks, water, lemonade, orange jui—"

"Maybe water." He walked out of the bathroom. "I..." He paused, sucked in a breath.

She did the same. Wowza.

"Forget the water." He started toward the bed. "I'm so glad you turned on the light."

"Me, too." That was putting it mildly. Sex in the dark with this guy? What had she been thinking? She'd hit the jackpot tonight.

"My imagination didn't do you justice."

"I know the feeling." With great effort, she tore her attention away from his considerable endowments and took the journey upward slowly, lingering on his six-pack abs and his broad, lightly furred chest. By the time she looked into his brown eyes, they were sparkling with amusement.

"Finished?"

"No, but I don't want to be rude."

He grinned. "My ego thanks you."

"My hoo-ha thanks *you*. Am I really the first woman in Wagon Train to get a full frontal?"

"Yes."

"It seems a shame. You were built for pleasure."

"That's what got me into trouble."

"Tonight it won't. You have my word."

"I believe you." His gaze heated. "Climb in and stretch out for me. I want to get to know you better."

Pulse racing, she obliged. Since he hadn't asked for another condom, clearly he had an alternative in mind.

Sliding in, he rolled to his side facing her, his head propped on his hand. Slowly he trailed a finger down the side of her cheek. "For one thing, I don't know your last name."

"You don't?" That startled her.

"I've only heard Brit."

Then again, he hadn't lived here long. "My last name is Powers. And I'm Brittany, with three syllables, but everyone calls me—"

"Brit. I know." Smiling, he looked into her eyes. "I happen to like Brittany. With three syllables."

She flushed. "So do I."

"It's beautiful, like you." He leaned down and placed a kiss on her forehead as he murmured her name.

Ahhh. She hadn't counted on being charmed, but it was her birthday. She'd take it.

His breath was warm on her face as he kissed her eyelids, then her cheeks, and finally claimed her mouth. She opened to him, hungry for all the stored up passion he had to offer.

While ravishing her mouth, he explored her body with a light touch, teasing her nipples, brushing her thighs, making silent promises of more delights in store. And then he dialed it up.

His lips and tongue followed the path of his knowing hands, seeking out every sensitive inch of her body, arousing her to a fever pitch. When she began to moan and whimper, he slid down and wedged his shoulders between her thighs.

Speaking her name softly, reverently, he bestowed the most intimate kiss of all. And drove her right out of her mind.

7

Brittany. Trent couldn't get enough of her. And she responded as if she couldn't get enough of him. After he'd thoroughly loved her from head to toe, she still had gas in the tank.

So did he. Grabbing another condom from the drawer, he plunged deep with a moan of delight. She rose to meet him, synchronizing her movements with his as if they'd been lovers for years.

They came within a split second of each other, laughing and shouting like kids at an amusement park. He'd never had sex like that.

But as he gazed down at her and gulped for air, he stopped himself from saying so. Instead he settled for a one-word comment. "Amazing."

"Sure was."

He soaked up the happiness in her blue eyes for as long as he dared and then left the bed to dispose of the condom. He could not, absolutely could *not* get hooked on her.

"I'm fetching us something to drink," she called out from the bedroom. "State your preference or you'll have to take whatever I bring you."

"Beer." He was in a party-hearty mood. Living for the moment.

"Got it."

When he walked out of the bathroom, she was coming in from the hallway, an open amber bottle in each hand. She hadn't bothered to put on clothes.

He grinned. "Best beverage delivery service I've ever encountered."

"Eat your heart out, Hooters." She handed him a bottle. "I thought we'd just drink them in bed."

"I'm for that." Scooting onto sheets still warm from enthusiastic sex, he propped himself against a couple of pillows. So did she. Then he tapped his bottle against hers. "Happy Birthday, Brittany."

"Thank you." She took a sip and glanced at him. "Are you really going to call me that?"

"Thinking about it. Do you mind?"

"No, but folks will comment on it."

"Probably. They'll think I'm a dork. Fine with me."

"Okay, then. I'll be prepared for it when we see each other in a week at Desiree and Andy's wedding."

So much for living in the moment. She'd already leaped ahead to the following Sunday. "They've invited most of the town. We might miss each other entirely." He didn't believe that for a minute. He'd locate her whether he wanted to or not.

"You might have to search for me because I'm short, but I'll be able to find you, no problem."

"I doubt it. All cowboys look alike."

"Not true. None of you wear your hats the same."

"Again with the hat?"

"It's true. Some tilt it forward, some push it back a little. You wear yours sitting squarely on your head."

"Next Sunday I'll tilt it. You'll never know I'm there."

She looked over at him, her gaze serious. "You know I will, hat or no hat."

"Just like I'll find you, even if you're trapped in a circle of tall people."

"So if we're bound to end up chatting with each other, calling me Brittany might be a good thing. It'll sound like you don't know me very well."

"In other words, you'd rather not have this escapade become common knowledge." He took a drink, using that to hide a prick of disappointment. He'd figured that would be the case.

"If it comes out, no biggie." She hesitated. "But since we're both acting out of character...."

"It'll cause a stir. Especially in your case. I'm still somewhat of an unknown quantity. They might think I'm just the type."

"No, they won't." She swatted him on the arm. "Everyone has you pegged as an upstanding guy. You should have heard Ella and Faye rave about you tonight."

"Will this ruin my reputation?" He gave her a look of mock horror.

"Just the opposite. It'll put the single ladies on alert that you've kicked off the traces."

He groaned. "And that's the biggest reason I don't want anything to get out. You said it yourself. I'm not ready. I may never be. I've lost my faith in happily ever after."

"Your parents seem to get along okay."

"They do." His chest tightened. "They also say it was dumb luck they happened to choose the right person. My mom told me that when I was going through my divorce. I think it was supposed to make me feel better, but it didn't." Time to change the subject.

"My mom believes the same thing. Unfortunately, she didn't luck out."

He glanced at her. "Your folks are divorced?"

"For more than twenty years. My mom's never found anybody she wanted to get serious about, let alone have another child with."

"Then I take it you're an only."

"I am. She would have loved to give me a sister or brother, but as she willingly admits, she's no Desiree McLintock. Going that route takes a woman strong enough to buck tradition."

"Her story's unusual."

"To say the least. She told me that searching for Mr. Right meant losing valuable time during her child-bearing years and she really wanted kids. I get that."

"Do you want some?"

"Sure do." She let out a wistful sigh. "I probably should have taken a page out of Desiree's book years ago. I'd probably still be single, but at least I'd have a couple of munchkins running around." She turned to him. "Did you want kids? I mean, before you and the clueless idiot split."

That made him smile. "You don't know that she's a clueless idiot."

"She divorced you. That's all the evidence I need."

Her kindness touched him, even though she didn't have nearly enough info to make that call. "Thanks. And yes, I wanted kids. She asked if we could wait a few years, which turned out to be a good thing."

Her gaze turned thoughtful. "Looks like we're in the same boat."

"I suppose. I've come to grips with it by deciding I'll be one hell of an uncle. Dallas and Angie are planning on giving Desiree another grandchild or two eventually. I also have two sisters, so one or both of them might have children."

"There's the rub for me. No siblings." She drained her bottle and set it on the nightstand.

"Doesn't have to be a sibling. I'll bet Ella and Marsh will be happy to share their baby with Aunt Brittany."

That perked her up. "They've already said so, which delights me. Faye and Gil are trying to get pregnant, too. They already refer to me as Auntie Brit. Aunt Brittany sounds so much better, though. I may push that agenda."

"In the end, the kids will come up with their own name for you."

"Yeah, they will." She smiled. "That's one of the things I love about them. They're so funny and creative." She stared into space, her breathing slow and steady. "I'll love watching Ella and Faye's children grow. They'll be part of my family, for sure." She turned to him. "But it's not the same as having my own, where I'm with them every day."

"No, it's not." Something was going on with her. An uneasy churning in his gut warned him that he wasn't going to like it.

She sat up straighter. "You'll think I'm nuts for what I'm about to say."

"I will?" More churning.

"Biologically speaking, time is running out for me. I want to have a baby before it's too late."

"I guess you could try a sperm bank." And he'd wager a sizeable sum she wasn't thinking that at all. He began to sweat.

"I don't like the sperm bank idea. I want to know my baby's father. I want to get pregnant the old-fashioned way."

"Which is great if circumstances are right for it."

"I think they are."

His gut clenched. "No, they're not."

"Yes, they *are*. I want to be a mother. You want to be a father. Why not—"

He pushed away from the pillows and stared at her. "You're really going to go there?"

"Yes, I am! It's the perfect solution to our problem."

He had no words. How could she suggest such a thing? Their carefree night of passion had just come to a screeching halt. Time to hit the road. "I'm sorry, Brit. That won't work for me."

8

In less than a minute she'd been demoted from Brittany to Brit. Not surprising. She'd been so excited by her idea that she'd said what was on her mind instead of leading up to it slowly.

By going straight to the point, she'd shocked the hell out of Trent. He was already out of bed and reaching for his pants.

"Wait."

He paused. "You were just kidding?"

"No, but—"

"Then I need to go." He put on his briefs and sat on the edge of the bed to pull on his socks. "This was supposed to be an uncomplicated deal, a *one and done* as you put it."

"That's all I intended, but then as we got to talking, it hit me. We both long to experience having a kid of our own, but neither of us trusts the concept of happily ever after. So why not follow in Desiree's footsteps?"

Standing, he put on his jeans, buttoning and zipping them with an air of finality. "You can certainly do that if you want. I wish you well. But I'm not your guy."

"Why not?"

He gazed at her. "You told me earlier I wasn't ready for a relationship and now you're suggesting I become a father? That doesn't compute."

"Those are entirely different things. In a relationship with another adult, you're dealing with each other's history, good and bad. It's tough to find someone you truly match up with. But with a baby, you start fresh."

"And right from the get-go, you have a million ways to screw it up." Propping his hips against the nightstand, he used it as support while he shoved his feet into his boots.

"But unlike most parents, who are trying to navigate their romantic relationship *and* raise a child, we'd be free to focus on the child. I see it as win-win."

He straightened. "I see it as a recipe for disaster."

"It doesn't have to be. Desiree is living proof that it works."

"Not exactly. All those dads were from somewhere else and they all moved away once they provided her with a child. Well, Angie's dad didn't move. He died. Point is, they didn't stick around."

"True."

"I'm planning to make an offer on the cabin I'm renting from Cheyenne, so if you're figuring on me leaving town eventually since I'm not from here, that's—"

"I'm not! I'd want you to be here, to share in the experience."

"What about custody? I'm pretty sure Desiree had sole custody of those kids. The guys had no responsibility, or rights, for that matter. That would never work for me."

"I understand and I agree. We should have joint custody. But we'd maintain separate households."

"That's crazy. And confusing for the kid."

"Is it? I grew up with the McLintock brood. They weren't confused. Children are more adaptable than we give them credit for."

He rubbed the back of his neck while he focused on a point just past her left shoulder.

Her pulse quickened. She hadn't won him over by a long shot, but at least he was thinking about it. She had more arguments, but maybe she'd be better off staying quiet for a while.

He sighed and met her gaze. "I still see land mines. What if you meet Mr. Right?"

"Then I'd marry him. If you meet Ms. Right, you'd marry her."

"More confusion for the kid."

"Not as much as you think. Divorced couples handle that contingency all the time. And their kids go through at least some trauma during the divorce. I certainly did when my parents split. Our child wouldn't have that issue."

"Our child." His soft murmur revealed equal measures of awe and disbelief.

"Has a nice ring to it, don't you think?"

"Gives me the shivers."

"Shivers aren't necessarily bad."

"They're not necessarily good, either." He shoved his hands in the pocket of his jeans. "You just threw me a hell of a curve ball, Brittany."

"I realize that." She warmed at the sound of *Brittany*, especially the way he said it. "Please don't make the decision now. Give yourself time to think it through."

"I doubt my answer will change. It's an interesting idea, but I can't see myself going along with it. The concept's way outside my comfort zone."

"Then maybe you're not as excited about being a parent as I am. I really want this, and suddenly I can see a way that doesn't involve finding the perfect spouse. Or taking potluck with a sperm bank."

"At least you have that second option. I only have the first, and evidently I suck at it."

"See? You're making my argument for me."

He shook his head. "I can't picture myself doing it."

"Not now. But maybe after the possibility has time to percolate, you'll see it differently."

"I don't think so."

"When do you work at the Buffalo again?"

"Tuesday night, with Rance."

"Do you usually close for him like you did tonight?"

"I do. It's my way of thanking him for getting me the job."

"Then how about this — I'll come by at closing time Tuesday night and we'll talk some more."

He held her gaze for a moment. Then his chest heaved. "Okay. But don't get your hopes up."

"I promise I won't. But if your answer is yes, we'll need to get started right away."

His breath hitched. "Why is that?" His voice sounded a little tight, as if he might be dealing with the mental picture she'd just created.

"It's my fertile time."

"You keep track?" The flicker in his brown eyes grew brighter.

"Not consciously, but it's a frequent topic with Ella and Faye, so now I know how to figure when I'm most likely to get pregnant. It's this week."

"I see." He swallowed, then stood there looking at her. "Good thing we used condoms."

"Definitely." Except that wasn't the message he was sending with his hot stare. She knew that look. Dollars to donuts he was envisioning having sex without those little raincoats.

He cleared his throat. "I'll be going, then. I just need to get my shirt and jacket." He stayed rooted to the spot, as if he was hoping she'd change his mind about leaving.

She wasn't about to seduce him into this decision. It wasn't a good way to start. She glanced up at the bedpost. "Don't forget your hat."

He blinked. "Right." Snatching it, he crammed it on his head and headed out of the room.

_9_

Physical exercise relieved the tension in a way nothing else could, so Trent spent Sunday morning mucking out stalls and cleaning tack. Whenever one of the McLintocks showed up at the barn, he laughed and joked with them as if he didn't have a care in the world.

In the afternoon he took Gigabyte out. He put a lot of miles on that gelding before finally bringing him back to his stall for a thorough rubdown. Desiree must have spied him riding in because she came to see him while he was brushing Gigabyte.

He politely turned down her invitation to have dinner at the ranch house. The meal he had cooking in his crockpot was a good excuse, but his real reason was that he needed time alone to order his thoughts.

Or not. After a mostly sleepless night, he admitted he couldn't make a decision about Brittany without talking to someone. He only trusted one person to give him advice on a life-changing issue like this and Dallas was on duty at the firehouse until Tuesday morning.

He slogged through Monday morning collecting data for a new client, and Monday afternoon he texted his brother at the firehouse, asking him to call when he had a chance.

Dallas responded within minutes. "Hey, bro, what's up?"

"I need to talk to you about...a problem I'm wrestling with."

"I'm all ears. Just be aware if a call comes in, I'll have to hang up."

"I'd rather talk in person. Do you and Angie have plans tomorrow?"

"Not specific plans, but she's taking the day off. We haven't spent much quality time together recently and we're both getting snarly about it. We'll be hiding out at the house, making up for lost time, if you know what I mean."

"I do." And he envied the hell out of his brother right now. "This is a big ask, but would you be willing to stop by here on your way home in the morning? I won't keep you long, I promise, but there's something I need to discuss."

"I can do that, or I could carve out some time on Wednesday. Angie has a wedding project she needs help with but I could get away for an hour or so if you need to talk. She'd understand."

"Wednesday's too late. I have to make a decision by tomorrow night."

"Is this about whether to make an offer on the cabin? Because I don't think Cheyenne's in any hurry to—"

"It's not about the cabin."

"I can't imagine — uh-oh, a call just came in. I'll stop by in the morning." He disconnected.

Trent slept better that night knowing he'd see Dallas in the morning. But he was awake before dawn and prowling through the cabin, a mug of coffee in his hand, his nerves raw, while he waited for his brother.

He could save himself this agony if he simply decided not to consider Brittany's plan. Then he wouldn't have to talk to Dallas. He could tell him the problem was solved and send him home to Angie.

Why wasn't he doing that? Because he *was* considering Brittany's plan. He couldn't put the concept out of his mind for more than five minutes at a time. He needed to bounce it off his big brother and get his reaction.

Finally he threw on a jacket against the cool May morning and took a refill of coffee out to the porch. The table and chairs on the far end belonged to Cheyenne. So did a fair amount of the furniture inside, since Cheyenne had moved into Kendall's fully furnished place.

If Trent bought this cabin, and he fully intended to, he'd see if he could purchase the furniture as part of the deal. He liked it. He and Cheyenne had similar tastes.

He eyed the chairs, started to sit in one, and changed his mind. He needed to keep moving. Pacing the length of the porch, he sipped his coffee and listened to the birds waking up in the tall pines on either side of the flagstone walkway.

The sound of a truck on the road brought him to a halt. He set his mug on the rustic table. Moments later Dallas's dark blue F-150 pulled in next to his tricked-out 250. The colors were similar, except his was a deeper navy with a pinstripe.

Rance had talked him into a fancy rig and he didn't regret it. Driving it always lifted his mood. But it had also set the stage for his current dilemma.

Opening his door and climbing out, Dallas called out a *hey*.

Trent did the same. "Can I get you some coffee?"

"Thanks, but I'll pass." He took the steps two at a time and shoved back his hat. "So what's got your undies in a bunch?"

"It's Brittany."

"Brit? Ella's friend?"

"Yep. I bartended Saturday night and she was at the Buffalo celebrating her birthday with Ella and Faye."

"Okay." Dallas gazed at him. "Then what?"

He rolled his shoulders and cleared his throat. "She left her purse and came back to get it. She'd walked there from her house, so I finished closing up and took her home. And then...." He glanced at his brother. "I slept with her. At her suggestion."

Dallas blinked. "I'll be damned. Well, that's probably a good thing. You— wait a second. Don't tell me you didn't use a—"

"I did. Both times."

"TMI, bro." His brother snorted. "But I'm happy for you. Are you going to see her again?"

"She's coming by after closing tonight, which is why I need to talk to you."

"What for? Sounds like things are going along just fine. Nice choice, by the way, not that you need my stamp of approval. Everyone likes Drit. She's a lot of fun."

"She wants to have my baby."

"She *what*?" Dallas's jovial smile turned to open-mouthed shock. "What the hell, Trent?"

"She wants a baby and hasn't found anybody she'd like to marry. She hopes to follow in Desiree's footsteps and have a kid anyway. With my help."

"You must have misunderstood. Was she drunk? I'll bet she was drinking those red, white and blues. Or she was pranking you. No way would she—"

"She was dead serious. She just turned thirty-one, and I can see her point. Guys don't have to worry about age so much, but women do. Then there's Desiree, who's demonstrated that a woman doesn't need a husband to have a bunch of kids."

"Desiree's an unusual woman. Not many could pull off what she did."

"According to Rance, Brittany's no ordinary lady, either. Nobody's equaled her stint as the high school mascot."

"The school mascot, huh? I didn't know that, but it fits. She's a bundle of energy. Maybe she has what it takes to work Desiree's program." His gaze sharpened. "Are you thinking of going along with it? Is that why I'm here?"

He nodded. "At first I told her no and hell, no. But she had some good arguments why it would be a solution for both of us. I don't plan to get married again, and—"

"Of course you don't. You're only six months away from that bloodbath. Eventually you'll heal. You'll regain your faith in love and you'll find a wonderful woman. You'll have those kids you want. I know you don't believe me, but—"

"You're right, I don't believe you. But let's pretend all that will come true. It's gonna take a while. Since I'd rather hang out with women my age, I'm in the same fix as Brittany. I'll be racing the clock."

"You keep calling her Brittany. Did she ask you to?"

"No, I just like it."

Dallas studied him. "And you like her."

"I do. I have a lousy track record regarding women, but I don't think she has a hidden agenda."

"Probably not. She and Ella have been tight ever since they were in grade school, which is a good sign. I've never heard anything negative about Brit. I like her, too. But do I think you should go along with this goofy idea? No, I don't."

"Are you saying that Desiree had a goofy idea when she conceived her kids this way?"

He opened his mouth. Closed it again. Shook his head. "She did what was right for her, but—"

"Were the dads of those kids idiots for going along with her plan?"

"I'm sure they had their reasons."

"Well, so do I."

"Only because Cheryl tore you to shreds. I know you've had it rough, but falling in with Brit's baby plan isn't the answer."

"I didn't think so either at first. I'm not surprised at your reaction. It made me argue from Brittany's point of view, which was helpful. Opened my eyes quite a bit. Thanks."

"I'm trying to talk you out of this, dammit."

"I know you are, and I appreciate the effort. I get why you're against me doing it."

"But you're going to, aren't you?"

"Looks like it."

Dragging in a breath, Dallas let it out slowly. "Then I'll support you."

His chest tightened. "Thanks, big brother. That means a lot."

"Who do you plan to tell besides me?"

"Brittany."

That brought a reluctant smile. "Besides her."

"I figure she and I will talk about it. I'll let you know what comes out of that. In the meantime, you can share it with Angie."

"You're okay with me telling her?"

"Are you okay *not* telling her?"

"No, but I—"

"That's what I thought. Just ask her to keep it to herself for now."

"She'll do that. But you'll run out of road pretty quick. Mom and Dad are flying in day after tomorrow."

"I know. I'll find a time to tell them, too. It's not like they'll spread the word."

"They won't, but eventually everyone will—"

"Assuming this works."

"Do you have any doubt?"

"No, not really." He couldn't explain why he was so certain, but he was. By the end of the week, Brittany would be pregnant. By the end of the month, he'd be a confirmed dad-to-be.

10

Normally Brit wasn't a nervous Nellie, but this situation with Trent had her spooked. Likely that was because she'd given him control of how it would turn out.

But what choice did she have? Without his participation, she had no immediate plan.

For the walk to the Buffalo she'd added a fleece vest to her outfit. She'd kept it simple — jeans, boots, a knit long-sleeved shirt and the vest.

Nothing about her said *take me big boy, I'm all yours* because she didn't want that sort of wild emotion connected with what should be a carefully considered decision. Yes, they'd had hot sex on Saturday night, but that shouldn't be the primary factor influencing him.

She wanted a committed father, not a man focused only on sex. Funny thing was, she could see him falling right into the committed dad role. Maybe that was why she'd come up with this idea in the first place.

Before she reached the Buffalo, she checked the time on her phone and paused in the shadows to see if any customers still lingered inside. Closing time on weeknights was eleven, but the Buffalo staff wouldn't kick people out if they stayed a few minutes after that.

From what she could tell, all the customers had left. Heart slamming against her ribs, she approached the front door with its frosted glass inset and knocked.

Trent opened it seconds later. "Hi."

"Hi." She stood there staring at him. Was he the answer to her dreams or a bitter disappointment?

"Come on in." He stepped back, a push broom in one hand. "I'm just finishing up."

And??? She curbed her raging impatience. If it were her, she'd have blurted out her answer the minute they came in contact after their explosive coupling and mind-bending discussion on Saturday night.

Trent wasn't like that. Duly noted. The sound system was on, and the song just ending was Chris Young's *It Takes a Man.*

The song was about pregnancy. Her breath caught. Was that a coincidence? Then *Lullaby* by the Chicks came on. Heart thumping, she turned to him. He gave a slow nod, and she lost it. Running across the floor, she threw herself at him, knocking the broom from his hands.

His strong arms tightened around her.

"Thank you," she blubbered, her throat tight. "You won't regret this."

His soft chuckle tickled her ear. "Wanna bet?"

She pulled back and gazed into those warm brown eyes. "You won't. I'll see to it."

"Don't make promises." He cupped her cheek. "This is uncharted territory for both of us. We don't know how it'll work out."

"I guess not. But I'm so grateful. I can't even begin to tell you—"

"Let me finish up, okay? Then we can get outta here."

"Okay." She eased away from him. "I'll just go twirl around on a bar stool."

"Do that." He grinned. "I'll only be a moment."

"Just so you know, I walked here."

"Then I guess I need to take you home." He said it casually, as if taking her home had no special significance. Picking up the broom, he went back to sweeping the floor.

"That would be lovely, if you don't mind."

"Not at all."

She perched on the bar stool but didn't twirl around. She was too busy looking at Trent, her knight in shining armor. The father of their child.

He reached for a dustpan and swept debris into it. "How was Glacier?"

"Gorgeous. We had a blast."

"Glad to hear it. I opened a college fund at the bank today."

"You're kidding."

"No, ma'am."

"But I'm not even pregnant yet."

"You will be."

His confidence made her shiver in anticipation. She couldn't believe he'd said yes, though. He'd been so dead-set against it when he'd left Saturday night.

"Why did you decide to do it?"

"My parents opened one for each of us when—"

"Not the account."

"Oh." He kept sweeping. "I talked to Dallas."

"And he was in favor?" That would be a shocker.

"Not even slightly. But arguing with him helped me see it was the right move."

"Is he upset?"

"He's not overjoyed, but he'll support me." He glanced at her. "Support us."

She gulped. "That's huge. I didn't stop to think about the reaction we'll get from friends and family. Will he tell Angie?"

"I told him he could, but to keep it between the two of them for now."

"I need to tell my mom."

"And I'll tell my folks while they're here for the wedding. You've met them, right? You must have. You made that comment about them getting along well."

"I did meet them. Liked them a lot. It's funny that I remember them from Angie and Dallas's wedding but I don't remember you."

"Probably because Rance was determined to find me dates and I was just as determined to sabotage his efforts."

"Are you planning to say anything to him? You two are close."

"I won't, not yet. I'd like to get past Desiree and Andy's wedding."

"Understood. I'm glad you'll have a chance to talk to your folks in person, though. I don't want this pregnancy to look like an accident."

He nodded. "I'm guessing your mom will want to meet me as soon as you tell her."

"She will. But don't be worried. She's not scary. If this is what I want, she'll go along."

"That's where Dallas stands. He thinks it's crazy, but in the end, he's on my side."

"Do *you* still think it's crazy?"

He stopped sweeping and looked at her. "It's totally insane. It's also the best idea I've heard in forever."

"Yeah?" Her heartbeat quickened.

"Yeah." His voice softened. "We'll have a great time making this baby."

The heat in his eyes set her on fire and she gulped for air. "Except it's not about having a great—"

"Why not? This isn't a science experiment. We're not combining elements in a test tube. We're going to create a baby the old-fashioned way. That's what you wanted, right?"

"Y-yes."

"So I'm gonna love the hell out of you for the next few nights and I'm really looking forward to it."

She trembled. "There's no guarantee it'll happen during that time."

"Are you saying I'll have to keep making love to you if we don't get it right? Damn, woman. If I'd known you were planning to put me through that kind of torture, I—"

"Stop it." She grinned. "I'm just trying to manage expectations."

"Then manage this. I'm in, whether it happens this month or not. We'll keep trying until we achieve the goal."

"Thank you for that." The prospect of additional attempts didn't bother her. Sounded like fun.

The glow in his eyes intensified. "But you'll be pregnant by the end of the week. And we both know it."

Her body clenched in response to the waves of sexuality rolling off him. Oh, yeah, she'd picked the right man for the job.

11

Trent was proud of his Oscar-worthy performance as the cool guy who was taking this gig in stride. He calmly put away the cleaning supplies and closed down the bar.

Then he escorted Brittany out the back door as if he hadn't considered grabbing her and having barstool sex before they left. Or up-against-the-wall sex. Or kitchen counter sex. He didn't need a condom so the sky was the limit.

But he'd controlled himself for fear he'd send her the message that sex was all he cared about. It wasn't true. He'd spent the entire day focused on his upcoming role as a dad.

He'd started with the obvious, researching the best sexual positions for making a baby, which predictably had stirred him up. To cool off he'd downloaded three parenting books and skimmed one. Then he'd rearranged his guest room to accommodate baby stuff. He'd checked out cribs, highchairs, playpens and car seats online.

By afternoon, the bewildering number of options had turned into shelf blur, so he'd hopped in his truck and driven to town. Besides opening a college savings account, he'd strolled the aisles of the Baby Barn.

He hadn't bought anything since hauling a teddy bear to work would be noticed. He could say it was for Ella's baby, or Jess's, since her second kid was due about the same time as Ella's first. Still, why create a situation where he had to lie?

Bottom line, he'd ended the day completely stoked about having a kid of his own. He could hardly wait. Nine months would be an eternity. He'd wanted this way more than he'd admitted to himself.

But the minute Brittany had walked through the door of the Buffalo, all baby dreams had taken a back seat to some extremely adult fantasies. He'd always had to worry about birth control. Always. Now the possibilities were endless. He and Brittany could have sex *anywhere.*

Before he handed her into the passenger seat of his truck, he resisted the urge to coax her into the back seat. The idea wouldn't go away. She wanted a baby ASAP. Might as well take every opportunity.

He tightened his jaw, closed her door and rounded the hood. Climbing behind the wheel, he laid his hat on the dash and winced as his cock protested being trapped in his jeans. He buckled up, determined to make it to her house and into her bedroom without succumbing to the lust surging through his body.

When he started the engine, the radio came on with Tim McGraw and Faith Hill's *Let's Make Love.* Talk about overkill. He reached for the power button.

She caught his hand. "One of my favorites."

He turned his hand to clasp hers and brought it to his lips. "I want you so much I'm shaking."

Her voice was husky. "Same here."

"Music like this—"

"Makes you ache?"

He brushed his mouth over her knuckles. "Yes, ma'am."

"Me, too. But... like you said." She took a quick breath. "This isn't a science experiment. And the music—"

"I'll leave it on." He lowered her hand to his thigh and let go. She left it there, the warmth adding to the pressure on his fly.

She was right about the music, though. It reminded him that he wanted more than sex from this lady. He wanted this baby, their baby, and he or she would be conceived with tenderness and love.

After he backed out of the parking space, he covered her hand with his. Her left hand. No ring. He hadn't been conscious of that before. He noticed it now. This was a brave thing she was doing.

Faith and Tim serenaded them all the way to her house, which made it a little more than a three-minute drive. He concentrated on the emotional lyrics. The last time he'd made this trip he'd told himself to leave emotions out of the equation.

He didn't have to do that anymore. Tonight he'd take the first step toward an experience that was all about emotion. Brittany had offered him a chance he'd thought was lost to him and he was grateful.

Was he also turned on more than ever in his life? Yep. That wasn't a bad thing. He subscribed to the totally unscientific belief that enthusiastic love-making would give them a better chance of creating their baby.

Her house looked different as he pulled up at the curb. Then it hit him. "You left the lights on."

"I did." She hesitated. "I also… well, you'll see."

"You did something special for me? When you didn't know what I'd decide?"

"What can I say? I'm an optimist. Mostly."

She'd gone out on a limb, way out. He squeezed her hand before letting go so he could turn off the motor. "I'm glad I didn't let you down."

"I was prepared for that, too."

"Oh, yeah? What was Plan B?"

"There's a big ol' bottle of my favorite wine sitting on my kitchen table."

The thought of her downing that bottle all by herself tore a piece out of his heart. "But instead of drowning your sorrows, soon you'll have to say bye-bye to your drinking days." He reached for the door handle.

"They were over once I asked you to do this."

He glanced back at her. "But we haven't even…." He trailed off as he looked into blue eyes filled with eager excitement. "You think it'll be tonight?"

"I do."

His body tightened, especially the part below his belt. He was locked and loaded. "So do I. Stay put. I'll get you down."

"That's incredibly gallant, but I can get in and out of this truck by myself."

"I know, but I enjoy providing that small courtesy." He smiled. "And in the months ahead, you may appreciate a helping hand."

"Why?" Then she got it and a flush bloomed on her cheeks. "Point taken."

She'd be an adorable pregnant lady—her big belly a smile-worthy contrast to her small frame. Would she let him see her naked when she was—

"Are we going in or not?"

He snapped out of his daze. "We're going in." He hopped out, shut the door and jogged around to the passenger side, despite the pain in his crotch.

When he opened her door she swung to face him wearing his hat. "You forgot something."

Cute as hell. He gazed at her, a warm squishy sensation in his midsection that had nothing to do with what was going on down lower.

"You look way better in it than I do." Gripping her around the waist, he lifted her out. He'd hefted hay bales that weighed more than she did.

And just like that, he had a concern. "Listen, I'm a big guy and you're a small woman. What if our baby turns out to be like me?"

She tipped her head back since the hat brim blocked her view of him. "I doubt that'll be a problem."

"Are you sure? I was more than nine pounds. I'm worried that—"

"Nature has a way of working those things out." Reaching up, she cupped his face. "You are a big guy. All over. And I handled you with no problem on Saturday night."

Flames licked at his privates. "Yes, ma'am."

"Let's not buy trouble, cowboy. Come inside." She held out her hand. "I think you'll like what I did in the bedroom."

He shoved the door closed and took her hand. "I doubt you can improve on what you did in there two nights ago."

"That was lame, starting out in the dark and then switching to bright light."

"I wasn't talking about illumination."

"You're very kind. But I can do better."

"So can I." And he couldn't wait to show this courageous woman how good he could be when he put his heart into it.

12

After walking into the house, Brit didn't race down the hallway flinging off her clothes. She ached for Trent even more than she had on their first night together, but she didn't want to rush into a moment she would remember for the rest of her life.

She paused to leave his hat on a rack by the door. He shrugged out of his jacket and she took off her vest.

After they'd hung up both things, he made no move to haul her into his arms, as if he understood tonight was different. Instead he held out his hand. The pace of his breathing increased the closer they came to her bedroom.

She was eager for him to see it. She'd spent her lunch hour in the lighting section of Miller's Hardware looking for alternatives to her nightstand lamps. She'd bought two strands of small paper lanterns, one to hang between the posts at the head of her queen bed and another to go between the posts at the foot.

The lamps were off, leaving the soft glow of the lanterns to bathe her favorite pale green sheets and creamy comforter. She'd turned back the covers. When she led Trent through the doorway, his quick intake of breath was exactly what she'd been going for.

She glanced at him. "Like it?"

His chest heaved. "I love it."

"I was tempted to put a chocolate kiss on the pillow."

"Don't need chocolate." Taking her by the shoulders, he turned her to face him. "But I do need a kiss."

"So do I." She melted into his arms and sighed as he tucked her against his aroused body. "More than a kiss."

"Coming up." He chuckled. "Literally." His lips claimed hers and his fingers splayed over the seat of her jeans. Then his grip tightened and he lifted her up, settling her against the promising bulge behind his zipper. She wrapped her legs around his hips and snuggled closer.

He gasped against her mouth. Carrying her to the bed, he lowered her slowly and followed her down, his fly wedged between her thighs, his tongue playing wicked games with hers.

Then he raised his head slightly, his breathing uneven. "You won't get pregnant with all these clothes blocking the path."

"Can you make them disappear?"

"Yes, ma'am." Easing away, he tugged off her boots and socks. He made short work of removing her clothes, pulling her shirt over her head and slipping off her jeans and panties in one smooth operation.

"You're fast."

"I'm motivated." He stood back and worked just as quickly getting rid of his clothes.

Lying sideways on the mattress, she propped herself on her elbows to watch his virile body emerge. Thank heavens he'd said yes. She quivered in anticipation as he kicked away his jeans and approached the bed.

Bracing a hand on either side of her, he leaned in and nibbled on her mouth. "I've been doing some research," he murmured.

"And?"

"Position might not matter, but deep penetration does."

She groaned. "Then do that. Immediately, please."

He nipped at her lower lip. "First I need you to scoot around and lift up so I can put a pillow under your sweet little tush."

"Yes. Right." She scrambled to comply. She'd heard that tip somewhere, too, but staring at his amazing attributes had fried every last cell in her hormone-soaked brain.

He picked up a pillow as he climbed in and slid it neatly under her. "Good." He moved over her, his hips brushing her damp thighs, his gaze locked with hers. "I've never done this without a condom."

"Me, either."

"I'm afraid I'll be more sensitive." He dragged in a breath. "And you need to come first."

"No problem. I'm on the edge already." Smoothing her hands down his muscular back, she clasped his taut buns. They flexed beneath her palms.

"Obviously I am, too. Especially when you touch me like that."

"If you don't want me to, I'll—"

"Oh, no, I want you to. I love feeling your hands on me. Don't hold back. I just don't know how this'll go since it's a new experience."

"I've been thinking about it all day, imagining how good it'll feel."

"Maybe too good. That's what worries me." He probed gently. "But it goes with the territory, so I..." His breath caught as he eased a little way in. "Wow."

"Yeah." Satin over steel. The combination put every quivering nerve on high alert. "That's...."

"Amazing?"

"Yep."

He held her gaze. "It's baby time." One firm thrust and he was buried to the hilt. Swearing softly, he went very still. "Don't move."

"'kay." But her body wouldn't listen. The contractions began against her will. "Sorry, sorry, *sorry....*" She arched into him with a wild cry as her body responded to his commanding presence with an orgasm that shook her like a rag doll.

With another muttered oath, he rode the crest of the waves, stroking fast, gasping for air. Chest heaving, he drove deep one last time. His body shook as he let out a loud, expressive groan and rested his forehead on her shoulder.

She dug her fingertips into his glutes, holding him fast, welcoming the riches he had to offer. Gradually his shudders stopped.

She lay beneath him and took a deep breath. Had the magic connection worked? She concentrated on the sensations in her body, trying to get a reading.

Raising his head he gazed down at her. "You're frowning. Are you unhappy?"

"I'm very happy. That felt absolutely wonderful."

"But you're frowning."

"Because I'm concentrating, trying to tell if I'm pregnant or not."

"Huh?"

"I don't feel that certainty I expected to. I don't think we accomplished it this time. I was sure it would happen right away at the first shot, since we're both so eager for it, but I guess not."

"But we might have. I don't think you can tell that when it's only been a couple of minutes since we—"

"My mom could. She said she knew exactly when she became pregnant with me."

"I hesitate to question your mom's claim, but I find that hard to believe."

"I don't. She's very in tune with herself, and so am I. Besides, the doc confirmed that it certainly could have been that exact time, judging from when I was born."

"Hmm."

"You don't believe it's possible."

"It seems far-fetched, but I'm a guy. I wouldn't say I'm in tune with my body. Except for just now. I was in tune and singing the *Hallelujah Chorus.* I could really get used to going without those little raincoats."

She smiled. "Wasn't that terrific? Maybe that's why I can't tell what's going on, baby-wise.

My lady parts are too busy celebrating the fun they just had."

"And will have again." He leaned down and kissed her softly. "I think you're supposed to stay still for awhile."

"I am. For like fifteen minutes or so."

"Maybe that's when you'll tune in and find out what's going on."

"I suppose that's possible, but from the way my mom said it, I think she meant the info was available almost instantly."

"But everyone's different."

"True."

"I'll go wash up." He climbed out of bed. "How about I bring us each something to drink?"

"Lemonade sounds great. Help yourself to a beer if you—"

"Lemonade for me, too. Beer could slow down my sperm."

She chuckled. "Really?"

"Really. We're both on the wagon, now."

"Okay, then. I wonder if anyone will notice during the festivities."

"Probably not."

"You're right. It'll be a madhouse." She treated herself to another view of his trip into the bathroom to wash up.

Moments later he reappeared. "Any insights?"

"Nope."

"Then you don't think you're pregnant."

"Not yet."

"What a shame. That means we need to do it again."

She laughed. "Yes, and we might even manage to last a few minutes next time."

"I'd like that. Something this good should be savored." He left to fetch their drinks.

"Agreed!" she called after him.

What was wrong with her? Instead of being disappointed, she should be overjoyed that she wasn't pregnant yet. Once that happened, she'd have no excuse to continue making love to Trent Armstrong.

13

Homemade lemonade. Trent could tell by the tiny seeds that drifted to the top after he poured it into two ice-filled glasses.

Did Brittany like to cook? Her well-stocked refrigerator, the cookbooks lined up on the counter and the number of utensils in a crock by the stove indicated she did.

She was also neat, judging from the tidy kitchen. The living room had looked cozy, too, although he'd been too focused on getting her into bed to pay much attention.

What about her job? It startled him that he had no idea what she did for a living although he'd spent some incredibly intimate moments with her. Dallas probably knew but he hadn't thought to ask.

Probably wouldn't have even if he'd thought of it. Dallas wouldn't be impressed that he had so little knowledge of the prospective mother of his child. Except he knew she'd be a good one.

He based that partly on her magnetic personality and her strong ties to the community, but also on her healthy relationship with her own mother. She wasn't afraid to tell her mom about this plan because she could count on her support and understanding. That said a lot about how she was raised.

But he should know what her job was, for crying out loud. He found a tray and put the glasses on it. Then he spied a ceramic cookie jar in the shape of an apple. Lifting the lid, he breathed in chocolate chips. Okay, those cookies were going along, too.

When he walked in with the tray, she'd propped herself up with a couple of pillows stacked against the headboard.

She took one look at the tray and started laughing. "You found the cookies."

"They found me. Did you bake them?"

"Yes."

"Are we allowed to eat them in bed?"

"Depends. Are you messy?"

He liked that answer. Yep, she'd be a good mom. "I'm a bartender. We're trained to avoid messes."

"That only tells me you won't spill your drink."

"I brought us each a plate. I promise to lean over it when I eat them. I also found coasters for the lemonade."

"So far, so good. I'm tallying up points on the dad scale."

"It's a little late for that. You could already be pregnant."

"I'm not."

"The night's still young." He carried the tray to her side of the bed and put down a coaster on the nightstand before setting the lemonade on it.

"Not really. We're creeping up on midnight."

"You getting sleepy?" He walked to the other side of the bed and deposited his drink and the tray.

"Not me. You?"

"Not a chance." He arranged his pillows the way she had hers and climbed in. Then he passed her a plate with two cookies on it. "You couldn't know this, but chocolate chip is my favorite kind."

"I'd be surprised if it wasn't. It's the favorite of more than ninety percent of the people in this country."

"Now you're talking like a marketing researcher."

"Which is what you do, right?" Head over her plate, she bit into her cookie.

"Yes, ma'am." He followed suit, making sure not to drop any crumbs. She'd taken the time to learn how he made his living. The minute he finished chewing this delicious cookie, he'd ask about her job.

"Ella said you're working on a project for Lucky, an expansion of the bookstore to another town."

He nodded. And took another bite. Couldn't help it. "Good cookies," he mumbled through a mouthful.

"Eat up. You need the energy. You're doing all the work while I just lie there."

"Hardly." He picked up his lemonade and took a long drink. Awesome lemonade, too. "And once the deed is done, you'll be doing everything while I loaf around." He'd meant to ask her a question. About what?

"Will you want to come to the doctor appointments?"

"Absolutely. And anything else you need a lift to. I checked out cribs and playpens online, but we could drive up to Missoula and see what they have. And car seats. We'll each need one of those." And he had a question about... something?

"Mom still has my crib and playpen, but I'll definitely need a car seat. The regulations have all changed."

"Your mom kept those things for you?"

"She did, and yes, that might be one of the reasons I'm so keen on having a baby."

"Because she's mentioned wanting grandchildren?"

"Never. She wouldn't want to imply it's my job to provide one. But I've seen how she looks at babies whenever we go somewhere together." She polished off her second cookie and picked up her lemonade. "I'm glad you brought those. I was too nervous to eat dinner."

"I wasn't all that hungry at dinnertime, either. The cookies hit the spot. Thanks."

Setting down her lemonade, she glanced at him. "I have stuff for breakfast, just in case, but we haven't talked schedules. How long were you planning to stay?"

"As long as you want. I'm self-employed."

"Well, I'm not, but I don't have to be at work until nine. Normally it's eight, but my eight o'clock cancelled."

That was what he'd wanted to ask! And she'd handed him the perfect opening. "What is it you do, exactly?"

"You don't know?"

"No, ma'am. I'm embarrassed to say I have no idea. I should have asked Lucky. Or Dallas. I failed to do that. I've heard you were a big hit as Casey Cougar. For all I know you've been hired to keep bouncing around the gym because they can't find a decent replacement."

"Nailed it." Her blue eyes gleamed with mischief.

"In that case, I want to see you in that outfit."

"That could be arranged. They gave it to me since the next Casey was a guy who was three sizes larger and the head didn't fit him, either. They presented it to me in a special ceremony after the last game of the year."

"Yeah, I need to see you in that."

"Now?"

"It can wait. But I still don't know what you'll be doing starting at nine in the morning."

"I work for Doc Bradbury."

"Ella's dad?"

"No, but you're not the first person to make that assumption. Ella's father is Doc Bradley, one of the last great general practitioners. Doc Elaine Brad*bury* is a dentist. I'm her hygienist."

"Bradley and Bradbury. What are the chances?"

"It's confusing. Sometimes newcomers think they're married to each other."

"So you're a dental hygienist." He automatically ran his tongue over his teeth. He hadn't been in for a cleaning since he'd left New Jersey.

"I recognize that guilty look in your eye. Don't worry. Your teeth are beautiful. Sparkling, even, which gets me hot. The grin you flashed me from behind the bar Saturday night dampened my panties."

That tickled him. He lowered his voice to a seductive murmur. "And they're all mine."

"Oooo, baby." She fluttered her eyelashes at him. "Do you brush and floss those sexy teeth?"

"I do." He gave her a slow, suggestive smile. "Regularly. Wanna watch?"

"Oh, yeah. Especially if you'll let me put my fingers in your mouth."

"Only if I can put my tongue in yours, pretty lady." And now he wanted to.

She met his gaze and her blue eyes darkened to navy. "Just your tongue? What about your—"

"I have other plans for that part of me." He shifted toward her and rose to his knees. Slipping his fingers through her luxurious dark hair, he cupped the back of her head and tilted her mouth up to meet his.

With a soft moan, she slackened her jaw and welcomed the thrust of his tongue. The sound brought an instant response from his cock.

As he continued to kiss the daylights out of her, she began a slow slide downward. He followed, keeping his body aligned above hers until she was lying beneath him, her thighs parted.

He had no trouble finding her warm, wet channel. When he glided slowly in, he thought his head would explode. A frantic pounding in his ears told him his heart was working overtime.

And he couldn't breathe. He lifted his mouth from hers and sucked in air. "This... this..."

"Is intense." Her breath feathered his damp lips and her fingers dug into the muscles of his back.

He didn't dare reach for a pillow. The movement could make him lose focus and come. Instead he engaged his core and tucked his hands under her, lifting her as he pushed deeper.

She gasped.

Bracing himself, he waited for her climax to erupt like it had before. When it didn't, he began to move, clenching his jaw as the pleasure mounted with each stroke. He had no words, only guttural sounds that blended with her soft, rhythmic cries.

He looked into her eyes and saw his own raw emotions reflected there. Her lips parted. She tensed. Then, with a wail, she came, her contractions rippling over his cock as he bore down.

He thrust once more, and again. Then he turned himself loose, driving in and holding on as his powerful spasms joined hers. He yelled like a man possessed.

Maybe he was a fool who'd end up with a ton of regrets. Worth it.

14

So relaxed. Brit lay quietly, every muscle in her body at rest, her heart thumping in a gentle rhythm. Trent gave her a tender kiss and left the bed slowly, as if he didn't want to jostle her and risk disturbing whatever was happening.

Or not happening. Calm settled over her, a light blanket of serenity that she'd never associated with sex. But then she'd never had this kind.

Mutual pleasure had always been the goal, the only goal, even with Trent on Saturday night. This time they'd had a different purpose and mutual pleasure had been a by-product. An unexpectedly lovely by-product.

The full-body orgasm she'd just enjoyed eclipsed any sexual experience she'd ever had. It left her sated, yet filled with joy and gratitude.

Her eyes drifted closed. The light click of plates being stacked and the whisper of bare feet on the floor told her he was taking the tray back to the kitchen. More dad points.

She was almost asleep when the mattress dipped as he crawled in beside her. Reaching for the covers, he drew them up, tucking them around her as if she were a child. "Do you want me to stay?" he murmured.

"Mm-hm."

"Do you think..."

Eyes closed, she slowly rolled her head from side to side.

"That's okay. We'll try in the morning."

"Mm-hm."

He kissed her again, his lips feather-light. "Sleep tight." Then he settled down with a deep, prolonged sigh of contentment.

The scent of coffee brewing roused her from the depths of a dream in which Trent rode toward her on a white horse. He carried a pink flag that rippled in the breeze. Gold letters proclaimed *IT'S TIME!*

What a nutty dream. She opened her eyes.

"About time."

She lifted her head and her knight stood at the foot of the bed wearing only his jeans, his arms folded over his impressive chest. The start of a beard shadowed his square jaw and outlined his tempting mouth.

A flash of white teeth when he smiled gave him a rakish air. "Good morning, princess."

She sucked in a breath. "Why'd you call me that?"

"You looked like Sleeping Beauty lying there. I kept checking on you 'cause I hated to wake you up when you were looking so happy and peaceful."

She propped herself up on her elbows. "I was having a really gonzo dream."

"About?"

"You were on a white horse and carrying a pink flag that said *it's time.*"

His eyebrows rose. "Well, now."

"How late is it?"

"According to the clock, it's sixteen minutes past seven. According to your dream, it's time to get busy making our daughter."

Heat flooded her lady parts. "It was just a dream."

"Was it? You're the one who's in tune with your body." He unfastened the metal button on his jeans and drew down the zipper. "I think your body was telling you something."

Her heart thumped faster. Her knight in shining armor believed in the power of dreams. That put him in a whole different category.

Stripping off his jeans and briefs, he strolled around to her side of the bed. "Are we on, princess?"

She gulped. "Sure, why not?" She tossed aside the covers.

"Good call." He moved over her, his brown eyes tawny in the morning light. "I'm not kissing you. You'd end up with razor burn."

"What if I don't care?"

"What if I do?" Bracing his forearms on either side of her shoulders, he eased between her thighs, his gaze intent. "This is perfect. You're relaxed and rested." He pushed in and gasped. "And ready."

Her breath caught as he went deeper. She was acutely conscious of his presence and his purpose. As he approached, she yielded, bit by bit.

"You're opening." His voice was husky. "You're opening to me. I feel it. I see it in your eyes."

She felt it, too. When the tip of his cock reached her womb, any remaining resistance melted.

Holding her gaze, he began to thrust, slowly at first, each time repeating that brief touch, keeping the drawbridge open and receptive. He increased the speed so gradually that her climax took her by surprise.

She arched into him with a startled cry as her body surrendered to the persistent demands of his.

"*Now.*" His strong voice rang out as he surged forward, gasping as he went deep one last time and locked into position, his cock rhythmically pulsing.

Her vision blurred, and for a few seconds she couldn't see his face through the mist. Was she crying? She blinked and tears dribbled from the corners of her eyes.

"Hey." He said it softly. Then he leaned down and brushed a kiss over her mouth. "I hope those are happy tears."

She looked into his warm brown eyes. "Uh-huh." She swallowed a lump in her throat. "We did it."

"Yes, ma'am. Congratulations."

"You believe me?"

"Have to. I was there. I felt it, too." His breath hitched. "At seven twenty-four a.m. Nine months from now we're gonna have a baby girl."

"You checked the time?"

"I wanted to know."

"We might not have a girl."

"Except it makes perfect sense. I was carrying a pink flag in your dream and it's up to me to bring the X chromosome."

"If you're right, just know I don't plan to dress her in pink all the time."

"Of course not. That's boring."

"She'll have a bunch of different colors to wear until she starts making her preference known."

"I think you're starting to agree that we'll have a girl."

"I suppose I am, even if I don't subscribe to that pink and blue stuff." She absorbed his slow grin. "Consciously."

"I promise not to buy a teddy bear with a pink bow." He paused, head turned, as if listening. "Coffee's done." He cautiously edged away and eased out of bed. "You need to stay here, so I'll start on breakfast."

"By yourself? That doesn't seem right."

"Sure it does." He retrieved his jeans and briefs. "I've done my part for this operation. While you do your part, I'll make sure we both get fed before we head into our day."

She focused on him, trying to get her bearings as her world began rearranging itself. She knew in her bones that they'd just created a child. They'd achieved their goal. What came next? She wasn't totally sure. "Okay. Thanks."

"You look a little dazed."

"So do you."

"I am. I know what happened, but I don't think it's sunk in yet."

"Same here."

"I'm sure it will." Breaking eye contact, he headed for the bathroom. "How do you like your eggs?"

"Scrambled, please."

"Well-done or moist?"

"Moist but not runny."

"Got it." He turned on the water in the sink.

She lay still and listened to him washing up. The rasp of his zipper signaled when he was done.

Moments later he reappeared. "I'll call you when it's ready. You should have plenty of time to make sure our girl is tucked in for the duration." He gave her a quick smile.

"I'll do my best."

"I'm sure you will." He left the bedroom.

He'd certainly done his best. He'd coaxed her to believe that her dream was a message from her body. Then he'd made sure that he'd responded to that message in a way that guaranteed success.

They both believed that they'd created a baby this morning. Which brought her to an inescapable conclusion.

They'd entered into this agreement to conceive a child, not become bed partners. With this morning's activity, they'd eliminated their only reason for making love.

_15_

Well, he'd done it, now. Trent set about cracking eggs and sticking bread in the toaster. He used six eggs because they hadn't discussed cooking up the bacon in the crisper drawer and he didn't want to add more cleanup when they were crunched for time.

She had to leave soon and he'd take off then, too. His truck parked at her curb had already been there long enough to arouse neighborly curiosity. But once he was out the door, once they'd said their goodbyes, would he ever be back?

Oh, sure, if he gave her a ride somewhere, or later when they were shuttling their daughter back and forth from her place to his. But he'd been too damned efficient, and now they'd completed the baby-making phase. The most incredible sexual experience of his life was officially over and he'd done it to himself.

If he hadn't agreed with her, if he'd cast doubt on her belief that they'd accomplished the goal, he might have talked his way back in. But he would have had to lie.

He knew in his heart and soul what had just happened. Barring the unexpected, they'd welcome a baby girl in nine months.

If he'd had a clue what making love to her would be like, would he have played this differently? Instead of being so damned confident they'd make it happen right away, would he have emphasized the difficulty of conceiving a child?

He was the king of research. He could have found plenty of stats to back up that premise. But no, he'd let his ego take control. If she wanted a baby, he'd give her one in record time because he was just that potent.

Congratulations, dummy. You just worked your way out of the sweetest job you've ever had.

"Trent?" Her voice drifted from the bedroom.

"Yeah?"

"Have you started the eggs?"

"Not yet." Because he'd been staring into space and cussing himself out.

"Would you please hold off for a bit? I'm going to jump in the shower."

"Sure thing!" He pictured her naked in the shower and groaned. He'd likely seen her naked for the last time about fifteen minutes ago, and he hadn't stopped to take a good look.

He'd just made love to her for the last time, too, and he hadn't paused a moment before leaving the haven of her body. He hadn't stopped to treasure the feeling of being cradled inside her warmth with no latex barrier between his skin and hers.

Instead he'd focused on the baby, their baby, which is what this was all supposed to be about. But he hadn't counted on the life-changing experience of making love to her coupled with sharing the excitement of conceiving a child.

He hadn't figured on the pleasure of that blowing him out of the water. Was it just because they hadn't used condoms? Or was it her special brand of lovemaking? Or did the magic come from the joy they created together?

He had no answers and was unlikely to get them in the future. He'd better quit feeling sorry for himself and be wearing a smiley face when she walked into the kitchen, because he'd landed himself in this position. It wasn't even slightly her fault.

She took longer in the shower than he'd anticipated and the eggs turned out crispy instead of moist. The toast sat too long so it was on the dry side, too. Butter helped, and he added some strawberry jam he found in the fridge.

"Sorry about the eggs." He set down both plates on her small kitchen table. "I misjudged the timing."

"No worries. Your timing was perfect where it counted."

He snorted. "Guess eggs are an appropriate breakfast this morning."

"Very."

"Have a seat. I'll get your coffee."

"Thanks, but I'm going to skip it."

"You are? Oh! I didn't even think about that. Is caffeine bad for the baby?"

"Ella's stopped drinking anything with caffeine in it, just to be on the safe side. Her dad said a little bit might not hurt, but she's not taking any chances. I don't want to, either."

"I'll get you some water, then. Will it bother you if I have coffee?"

"By all means have some. It smells delicious. I'm glad you made it because the smell is half the reason I love it." She slid into her seat and picked up the napkin he put by her plate.

"Do you have any decaf? I could make—"

"I don't have any. I'll pick up some today. I should have thought of it yesterday, but I was focused on buying those little lanterns."

"They're beautiful." So was she, with her hair in a jaunty ponytail and her cheeks flushed, which brightened the color of her eyes. She smelled like lilacs. "Will you leave them up?"

She dropped her attention to her plate and picked up her fork. "Probably not."

His heart sank. She was moving on. He started eating, although he had no appetite. When would he see her again? What excuse could he manufacture? Then he hit on a legitimate one. "What do you want to do regarding your mother?"

That brought her head up. "I've been thinking about that. I'll see her shortly. She's Doc Bradbury's office manager."

"That's convenient."

"She's the reason I have that job. I used to commute to Missoula, but Mom found out in advance the Doc's hygienist was leaving and I was the first and only applicant."

"That's great."

"Sure is. We work well together. Anyway, I should have a chance to talk to her this morning. We usually take a quick break for coffee."

"Which you won't be drinking."

"Right." She paused. "It's short notice, but can you meet us for lunch today at the Buffalo?"

"Sure can." Only a few hours away. "What time?"

"We close the office between noon and one-thirty, so we can be there around twelve-fifteen, which'll give us almost an hour."

"I'll show up a little early and get us a table. What's your mom's name?"

"Margaret. She'll want you to call her that instead of Mrs. Powers."

"She's not Margie or Marge?"

"No, she likes Margaret."

"Three syllables?"

She smiled. "Yep. Although most people slur over the middle one. She called me Brittany until I started school. Then everyone started calling me Brit, so eventually she did, too. Listen, if you want, you can shower here so you don't have to drive home and come back."

"Thanks, but I'll shower at home. I don't mind the drive and I'd like to put on clean clothes."

She studied him. "We need to talk and sort out a few things. But I have to get going."

"I'm available anytime you want me." Which was a little too on-the-nose, but the absolute truth.

Her gaze flickered. "It's not fair for you to do all the driving."

"Then come to the ranch sometime." But she'd need a reason. "You should check out my place, since our baby will be staying there once she's old enough."

She didn't answer right away, just sat there looking at him. Then she took a quick breath. "Good idea. My last client's at three-thirty. I should be done around four-thirty."

"Then come out for dinner." He tamped down the excitement churning in his gut. "Just dinner."

"That's what we need to talk about. We've shared something special, but now—"

"I get it. You're pregnant. Mission accomplished."

She made a face. "You're upset."

"No, I'm not."

"Yes, you are, and I don't blame you. I'm not feeling all comfy cozy, either. We need to discuss how things will be going forward and figure out what we plan to say once we start letting our friends and family know about the baby."

"Which'll be after the wedding, so no rush on that."

"Except your parents will be here tomorrow."

"Oh. Yes, they will." He and Dallas would be driving to Missoula to pick them up at the airport. His head wasn't in the game. It was still in the previous game.

"I have to go brush and floss before I leave." She pushed back her chair and stood.

"That's funny."

"Professional pride. Just leave the dishes. I'll handle them when I—"

"You're coming out to my place after work, remember? Go brush your teeth so you can skeedaddle. I'll take care of this."

"Thank you." She held his gaze for a moment. "You're great, Trent."

"So are you, Brittany." Rance had told him she was special. Dallas had praised her, too. They didn't know the half of it. But he did. He'd been given a brief glimpse of heaven.

And now he was in hell.

_16_

Brit loved her job and usually had no trouble focusing on it. Not this morning. She managed to do a thorough job of removing plaque from Joanie Ledbetter's teeth, but maintaining her concentration had been tough.

She'd already given her mom a heads up that they needed to talk during the break. Often they each grabbed their phones and used the time for answering calls or texts, but they'd have to skip that routine this morning.

Her mother arrived in the break room ahead of her and had already poured coffee for each of them. Brit took hers because explaining why she wouldn't be drinking it would start the conversation in the wrong place.

Her mom looked especially pretty this morning, and happy, too. Last week she'd had her hair cut shorter to take advantage of her natural curl and she loved the new style. At fifty-six she had a salt and pepper look going on and had decided not to color the silver, at least not yet.

She smiled when Brit walked in. "So what's up?"

Brit looked into eyes the same color as hers. "You might want to have a seat."

Her dark eyebrows rose. "Why?"

"I have big news. On Saturday night, or more like Sunday morning, I made a decision and it's worked out the way I hoped it would."

"Sunday morning? During our trip to Glacier?"

"No. Before that."

"Oh." Her gaze sharpened, a question hanging in the air.

"I didn't want to tell you until I had something definitive to report."

"Maybe I will sit down." She took a chair at the small round table.

Brit sat across from her and put down her coffee. "I decided not to wait until I'm married to have a baby. So I—"

"You went to a sperm bank? I would have gone with—"

"No sperm bank. I found a better option."

"What option? You're not even dating anyone!"

"No, but I found the perfect father for my child."

"In three days? Don't tell me you got him online. You can't trust—"

"He's right here."

"Here?" She spun around as if he might come through the door behind her.

"In Wagon Train. I wouldn't go online to get a baby-daddy, Mom. Sheesh." This wasn't going at all the way she'd scripted it in her head.

"It's more plausible than finding one in three days in this tiny town! You know all the eligible men and none of them have suited you so far. I can't imagine who—"

"Trent Armstrong."

"Who?"

"He's Dallas Armstrong's brother. Dallas is—"

"Okay, I know Dallas. He came in for a cleaning before his wedding, which I didn't get to because I had the flu. Was his brother there?"

"He was the best man. He's lived out at Rowdy Ranch since January."

"Have you been seeing him and failed to mention it?"

"No. But we crossed paths on Saturday night, and one thing led to another."

"You had unprotected sex with someone you hardly know?"

"Not then. And it's not like he's a total stranger. Ella and Faye think he's great."

"They know about this plan?"

"Not yet. You're the only one I've told so far."

"Well, thank God you told me before you launched into it. I understand the urge to have a baby. Believe me, I understand it very well, but—"

"Mom, I have launched into it. I asked him and he agreed. Trust me, this will work."

"Why are you so sure?"

"We have a similar issue. I want to have a kid before I get any older. He's divorced and says he'll never marry again, although he's sad about not having any kids. We're in the same boat, which is why I came up with the idea."

Her mom digested that before taking a breath. "I probably shouldn't be surprised. I wondered if it bothered you that Ella's pregnant."

"I won't lie. It's a factor. But I don't want to marry someone just to have a baby. This is a much better option."

"It's reminiscent of a Desiree McLintock move."

"That's exactly what it is. She's the one who inspired me to take this step."

"She suggested it?"

"Oh, heck, no. I can't imagine her ever doing something like that. But she's been on my mind this week because of her wedding. Then suddenly Trent shows up in my life — the perfect candidate."

"He'll give you custody? Because that's how Desiree worked it."

"We've agreed to share custody."

"That makes it a lot more complicated. The men Desiree chose didn't hang around. This guy has a brother here, so he may not ride conveniently off into the sunset."

"He doesn't plan to. He wants to be part of the baby's life."

"Uh-huh, like I said, complicated. You might want to give this plan a little more thought before you climb back in bed with him. I doubt you're pregnant yet. That only happens in the movies."

"Although—"

"Seriously, a couple of times won't do the trick. You still can back out. Am I the only one who knows?"

"You and Dallas. Trent told him yesterday."

"And what was his reaction?"

"He wasn't thrilled, but he'll be supportive."

"So will I, if you're sure this is right for you, but it seems really fast, honey. I wish you'd give it more thought."

Time to shift the conversation. "I'd like you to meet him."

"When?"

"Today for lunch at the Buffalo, if you're okay with that."

She blinked. "At the Buffalo? How long have you lived in Wagon Train?"

"All my life."

"Then surely you've noticed that what happens at the Buffalo doesn't stay at the Buffalo. I guarantee one of my friends will see us and ask me if Trent's your new boyfriend. What do you want me to say?"

"I don't know. Trent and I haven't worked out how we'll explain our relationship."

"If you abandon the idea now you won't have to explain anything."

"We're not going to abandon it."

Her mom gave her a long look. "Then I'd better meet him. Have you talked about living arrangements?"

"They won't change. He'll continue to stay out at the ranch and I'll have my house here in town."

"What about your personal relationship with each other?"

"We'll be friends."

"Friends with benefits?"

"No, just friends."

Her mom gazed at her. "And he's agreed to that?"

"Yes."

'Then I'm going to guess the sex was terrible and your only reason to have it is to make this baby you both want."

Heat rose to her cheeks. "Um, that's not exactly the case."

"You've both had fun?"

"Yes." She cleared her throat. "And the last time... this morning... I felt... I felt it happen."

Her mom gasped and her eyes widened. "You think you're already *pregnant*?"

"I'm sure I am. So is he. It's my fertile time and it was just like you described when you conceived me. I just knew."

"Oh, Brittany."

The use of her full name and the deep concern in her mother's eyes crushed her. "I thought you'd be happy."

"About the baby? Of course I am. For years I've dreamed of being a grandmother, but—"

"You don't sound happy."

"Honey, you've rushed into this with a man you don't know and I just... I don't see how that's going to work out."

"It can, Mom. I know it can. Trent's a good person, and if we avoid getting tangled up romantically, we'll be fine."

"You think that's possible?"

"Why not? Desiree managed it. She's good friends with all those guys and that's all they are, just friends. I've heard her say that."

"She does say that, but...." Her mom looked even more troubled than before.

"What?"

"You were a kid when Desiree was having those babies. I think you missed an important part of the story."

"Which part?"

"She fell passionately in love with each of those men."

"You mean temporarily? Like for a few days? Because I can see—"

"Not days. Months. They'd go dancing at the Buffalo, gaze into each other's eyes, hold hands walking down the street. It was obvious she was crazy about each one and they were crazy about her."

"Oh." She gulped. "I didn't hear that. So... then what?"

"Every time my friends and I would think *oh, she's finally found a guy she'll stick with.* Then next thing we knew, he'd be gone."

"She sent them away?"

"No, but this is Wagon Train, so eventually the story would come out, often because the guy himself confided in someone over a beer before leaving town."

"If she didn't make any of them go, why did they?"

"Some loved the sex but didn't fancy being a dad so they took off before the baby was born.

Looking back on it, I'll bet she picked them because of that. But at least two, maybe three, proposed to her. When she said no, they left to find a wife."

"I see." Not what she'd pictured at all.

"I'm sorry, honey. If I'd known you were thinking about doing this...."

"I wasn't until Sunday morning. Then it seemed like a brilliant solution." And it still would be, damn it. She and Trent would work this out.

"I take it you're not passionately in love with Trent?"

"No! And he's not in love with me, either. That's exactly what we plan to avoid. It would ruin everything."

"I only ask because it sounds like you two started a fire." She reached across the table and squeezed Brit's arm. "It won't be easy to put out."

17

   If Trent had been thinking straight, he would have suggested a different setup for meeting Brittany's mom. She could have come out to the ranch with her daughter tonight.

   That would have served a dual purpose. The meeting wouldn't be taking place in public and they'd have a chaperone. The way he was feeling every time he thought of Brittany, they'd need one.

   But an alternate plan didn't occur to him until he walked into the Buffalo a couple of minutes past noon. Maybe he hadn't thought of it because if he was totally honest with himself, he didn't want a chaperone tonight.

   On the other hand, a private meeting with Margaret Powers would have been way better than this very public venue. The minute he came through the door he caught sight of Desiree and Andy having lunch.

   Desiree looked up and waved. He waved back as he walked past the wooden mascot. Its greeting for the entire week was *Haaaapy Muuuther's Daaay.*

   He'd heard it quite a bit on Tuesday night before Brittany arrived and he'd learned to tune it out. Now those words evoked the passion-drenched episode that had ended at seven-twenty-four a.m., when everything changed.

He wasn't the same man who'd left the Buffalo last night. Was it written on his face? He hoped to hell it wasn't, because courtesy demanded that he go over and say hello to the happy couple.

And they looked pretty darned pleased with themselves as they sat across from each other at a two-top munching on burgers and sipping frosted mugs of cider.

Desiree motioned him over. "We were just talking about the Apple Grove project. Lucky's so excited about the grand opening of the bookstore next month."

"He should be. The demographics look good. With the Buckskin Ranch and the Choosy Moose supporting it, the word will get out, especially when they'll carry signed copies of M.R. Morrison's books."

Desiree nodded. "Those signed copies do well for us here, that's for sure."

"I just wish Morrison would agree to an in-person signing, but so far Lucky says the chances are slim to none."

"Don't give up hope." Andy glanced across at Desiree. "It could happen."

Desiree sighed. "Says the eternal optimist."

"Oh, I think we're making progress on that front," Andy said. "Can I get you a chair so you can join us, son? I assume you're here to grab some lunch."

"I am, and thanks for the invitation, but I'm meeting a couple of people. I told them I'd come early and get us a table."

"Then by all means do that. The place is filling up fast. We'll see you Friday night for the 'rehearsal'." He made air quotes.

Desiree laughed. "Which we do *not* need after all the weddings we've helped organize lately, but whatever."

"I'll be there."

"Good." She smiled at him. "I'd tell you to bring a date, but Rance informed me that's a non-starter."

"That might be changing a bit."

"Oh?" She brightened. "Then you might bring someone?"

"I might. See you then." He headed back toward the bar to find Cecily and secure a table.

He was making this up as he went along, but he figured everyone would take the news better if he and Brittany started showing up together, even if they billed it as a *just friends* situation. Viewed that way, maybe this lunch with her mom was exactly the right move.

Cecily grinned as he walked toward her. "I was about to chase you down to ask if you need a table."

"I do. For three people."

"Anyone I know?" She picked up three menus from the stack on the bar.

"Yeah, me."

"Smartass. Who'll be joining you?"

"Brittany and her mom."

She did a double-take. "Number one, everyone calls her Brit, FYI, and number two, why are you having lunch with her and Margaret? It's none of my business, of course, but it's a curious combination."

"I agree. And I'm not going to tell you why I'm having lunch with them."

"Fair enough. Do you want a table toward the back where it's a little more private?"

"Yes, please."

"Something's afoot. I can smell it."

"I knew this aftershave was too strong."

"Your aftershave is just right. So's the pale green shirt with the pearl buttons. Looks awesome on you. Are those new Wranglers?"

"Never mind."

"Come to think of it, I've never seen that shirt, either. And your boots are polished. Are these your Sunday go-to-meetin' clothes, Trent, darlin'?"

"Just show me to the table, please."

"Yes, sir." She winked at him. "Anything for you, Mr. Armstrong, sir."

"And I thought Rance was a pain in the ass."

"I taught Rance everything he knows about being a PITA." She walked toward a table in the far corner near the windows. "Well, that's not quite true. He picked up a lot from Beau before I got ahold of him. Does Rance know about this lunch?"

"No, and I'd appreciate it if you wouldn't tell him when he comes in this afternoon."

"What's it worth to ya?"

"Dammit, Cecily."

"I'm just funnin' ya, cowboy. I won't tell Rance. But if you didn't want anyone to know, you could've picked a better place than the Buffalo during the noon rush."

"Not my choice, but you're right."

She gestured to the corner table. "This is as secluded as it gets. Want me to bring you a shot of whiskey to calm your nerves?"

"What makes you think they need calming?"

"Oh, I dunno. The fact that you snatched the menus out of my hand and laid them at each place, like that was your job. Which it so isn't."

He glanced at the table. Sure enough. And he hadn't been aware of doing it. "The whiskey is a great idea but I don't have time to get sufficiently toasted. They'll be here any second."

"I can't wait to hear how this turns out."

"Me, either. But you need to let Janice wait on us. This is her section."

"All except this table."

"Uh-huh."

She patted his shoulder. "You need me here for backup in case things get hairy. I'll fetch three waters."

"Thanks." After she left, he chose the chair in the corner so he'd see them coming. He'd no sooner settled into it than they walked through the door, Brittany leading the way, ponytail swinging, and Margaret right behind, scanning the room. She was slightly taller than her daughter and had the same trim, athletic figure.

Eventually her gaze settled on him and she leaned toward Brittany to say something. She glanced quickly in his direction and nodded. He stood as Cecily brought them to the table, her tray loaded with three water glasses.

When they got there, Brittany's mom held out her hand. "Hello, Trent. I'm Margaret." No smile, but no frown, either.

"Nice to meet you, Margaret. Brittany mentioned you'd want me to use your first name."

Her brows arched. "Brittany? You call her that?"

"I know everybody calls her Brit, but I like the longer version."

"So do I." A faint gleam of approval flashed in her eyes, blue like her daughter's.

Remembering his manners, he quickly pulled out each of their chairs as Cecily set down the water glasses.

"Hey, Cecily." Margaret had a smile for *her.* "How's that puppy doing?"

"Growing like a weed. Does everyone need a minute?"

"I don't," Margaret said. "I'll have the Reuben, please. And coffee."

"Make that two." Brittany handed over her menu. "And decaf coffee for me, please."

"Make it three." Trent held out his menu. "And leaded for me. Thanks, Cecily."

"Be back in a flash." She gave him a glance of support and whisked away.

Margaret spread her napkin in her lap before glancing at him. "Brit told me you moonlight at the bar and by day you're a marketing consultant."

"That's right."

"And I hear you have a horse and pitch in doing ranch chores."

He glanced over at Brittany. "Did I tell you about Gigabyte?"

"About *what*?"

"My horse. I don't remember—"

"You didn't. That's a clever name. Faye told me you had one and that you help out around the barn."

Margaret looked over at him. "Busy guy. You must not have much free time."

He met her gaze and kept his steady. "The bartending is optional. I don't need the money, but I have fun doing it. I can give it up if time becomes an issue."

"Which it always does when you're the parent of a young child. Brit said you also believe there's a baby on the way."

"I do. I'm very happy about that."

"I'm glad you are, because it's a big responsibility."

"Which I take seriously."

"That's good to hear, too." She paused to take a sip of her water before turning back to him. Her expression softened. "How do you feel about my daughter?"

His breath hitched. Loaded question. "What do you mean?"

"Do you have an emotional attachment to her?"

"Of course. She's our baby's mother."

"And what emotions does that connection inspire?"

"Gratitude, protectiveness, caring, admiration. I'm sure there are more if I have some time to think about it."

She nodded. "That's a list to warm a mother's heart." She hesitated, then looked him right in the eye. "What about passion?"

"*Mom.*"

His throat clogged and he had to clear it. "No worries. It's a fair question, considering." He had a hunch the subject had already come up during her discussion with Brittany. "Making a baby should be passionate, and it was."

"Brit says you'll just be friends from now on and you've agreed to that."

"I have."

She took a quick breath. "I've already said this to Brit. But do you think that's realistic?"

"Three Reubens, coming up!"

He could have kissed Cecily. Well, not really. And it sure wouldn't help his cause to plant one on their server.

Her timing was impeccable, though. She must have seen the look on his face, because instead of delivering the meal with her usual brisk efficiency, she took forever.

She made sure they all had condiments, utensils, more water, cream and sugar for the coffee, and a sugar substitute if anyone needed that. She even hung around to find out if the Reubens were satisfactory and the coffee was the right temperature for everyone.

He used the time to get his bearings. When Cecily finally walked away, he was ready. She was so getting a big tip.

He turned to Margaret. "This is an unusual situation and I'm only human. But we agreed to a plan and we'll stick with the plan. We got together to have a baby, not to become lovers."

"You're right that it's an unusual situation. Extremely unusual. And I have one more question."

"Let's have it."

"What about love?"

Fortunately, he had an answer for that one. "You mean the happily-ever-after, romantic kind of love?"

"Yes."

"I used to believe in that. I don't anymore."

"How can that be when your brother just got married? And last time I checked, all but one of the McLintock boys have found their soul mates."

"It looks that way."

"Even Desiree, who's spent the past thirty-plus years avoiding a walk down the aisle, is getting married on Saturday. At Rowdy Ranch, you're surrounded by evidence that true love exists."

"I hope for their sake it does. But I'm not willing to take that gamble ever again."

She sighed. "Well, your attitude toward love and marriage is why Brit chose you for this crazy escapade. Maybe she knows what she's doing, after all."

"I believe she does."

Evidently Margaret had run out of zingers. Although she continued to fire off questions about his family, his job, and his child-rearing philosophy, none of them made his gut clench.

She had a right to question him. He'd be the father of her first grandchild, maybe her only grandchild, and she hadn't known he existed until today.

In her shoes, he'd be doing the same thing. In fact, he might be in her shoes someday, interviewing a randy teenager who wanted to date his daughter.

He could put himself in that mythical teenager's shoes, too. Whenever he looked at Brittany, flames licked at his privates. No doubt her mom had picked up on his ill-disguised obsession. Mothers were good at spotting that kind of behavior.

He could sit there insisting that this platonic friendship was going to work. His body didn't believe a word of it. And neither did Brittany's mother.

<u>*18*</u>

"He's a good-looking man, Brit, but he has a terrible attitude about love and marriage."

"For me that's a plus." Brit walked faster to keep pace with her mother's stride on the way back to the office. They weren't late, so there was no reason to barrel down the sidewalk, but her mom had a bee in her bonnet, as Grandma Hutchens used to say.

"But to be so jaded at such a young age just isn't right How old is he, anyway?"

"I'm surprised you didn't ask him."

"Didn't think of it. It doesn't matter. He's younger than Dallas and older than his two sisters, which makes him a middle child. Maybe that's his problem."

"Middle children have a problem?"

"Some do. They don't get the honor of being first or the spoiling of being last. But Trent doesn't seem to crave attention. I deliberately made lunch all about him and he kept trying to turn things around and find out more about me."

"Which he did! I had no idea you played softball in high school, let alone that you were team captain. Do you have pictures?"

"Somewhere. Remind me and I'll dig them out. Anyway, Trent seems like a good guy, not full of himself, but not shy, either. He's just lost his faith in finding a life partner. Completely lost it."

"Which means his ex smashed his heart into a million pieces." Hers gave a sympathetic tug.

"And he's been divorced how long?"

"Six months since the actual decree. I don't know how long they were separated before that."

"Likely several months or more. The process takes a while. By the time your dad's and mine was final, he was living with Rhonda. They got married the next week."

"And lived unhappily ever after. I know Dad likes me to visit, but it's no fun listening to them argue. They do it constantly."

"And have for twenty years. I'm glad they moved to Idaho, but I'm sorry your visits there are miserable." She sighed. "You haven't had good role models in the love and marriage department, honey. No wonder you decided Desiree had the right idea."

"Do you know why she didn't accept any of those proposals?"

"According to the scuttlebutt, Sky's father was the love of her life. But he broke up with her because he fell for someone else and she never told him she was pregnant. No man since then has measured up."

"Until Andy."

"He might not have measured up at thirty. He'll need all the patience and wisdom he's gathered over the years to deal with an independent woman like Desiree."

They'd reached the front door of Doc Bradbury's office but Brit made no move to go in. They had ten minutes left and the conversation was important. "But you said she fell madly in love with each of the dads."

"She did, but I guess not enough to marry them. She set a high bar when it came to matrimony." Her mom held her gaze. "Like you."

"Do you think that's a mistake? Am I too picky?"

"Not at all. I wasn't picky enough when I met your dad. In my heart I knew he wasn't fully committed. Then again, neither was I. Everyone around us was getting married so we did, too. That's not a good reason."

"I couldn't have said it better. Thank you. That's why I'm still single."

"And pregnant."

"Marriage doesn't have a timetable. Childbearing does."

Her mom looked as if she had a comeback, but she didn't say it. Instead she took a long, slow breath. "I get it. I tried like crazy to get pregnant again after you were born. I felt the clock ticking, too. But nothing happened."

"And there I was, begging you constantly for a brother or sister. I'm sorry, Mom." She gave her a hug.

"It's okay, sweetie. At least you stopped pestering after your dad and I split up. But I still thought about it, still wanted another baby, for you but also for me. Except I was too traditional. I couldn't picture having one on my own."

"Neither could I. Until I met Trent."

Her mom glanced around, clearly checking for potential eavesdroppers. Then she lowered her voice. "I can see why you chose him. And why he said yes. You two give off sparks like firecrackers on the Fourth."

She flushed. "That's a byproduct. It will fade."

"Keep telling yourself that. Have you seen how he looks at you?"

Her cheeks grew hotter. "He'll get over it." But would she?

"Not any time soon, honey. That man is besotted. He—"

"We should probably go in." Reaching for the door, she held it for her mom, who let out a sigh as she walked through it.

Brit followed and paused to take a calming breath. She didn't need to be reminded about the hot glances Trent had sent her way when he thought she wasn't paying attention. Or how eagerly her body had responded.

She'd better cancel the plan to drive out to the ranch after work. It was too soon. She'd text him when she had a few spare minutes.

But those few spare minutes never materialized. When she finally grabbed her phone at four-thirty, she found a text sent two hours ago with directions to his cabin and a message — *hope you like spaghetti. I'm making Marybeth's recipe for the sauce.*

She couldn't cancel on a guy who'd devoted time to homemade spaghetti sauce. It would be a good test to see how they'd manage this friends-only plan. Besides, his parents were flying in tomorrow and they hadn't talked about what he'd tell them.

After freshening up at home, she climbed in her truck, a modest two-seater with a short bed as opposed to Trent's massive F-250. She'd considered bringing a jacket but decided against it. She didn't need one for the short walk from her truck to his front door.

Country tunes might jumpstart her libido, so she searched on her phone for a podcast that dealt with healthy eating during pregnancy. Podcast playing, she headed out to Rowdy Ranch. No country tunes this trip.

She hadn't changed clothes or done anything different with her hair. This wasn't a dinner date. It was merely a chance to scope out Trent's cabin and discuss how they'd handle their new status.

The podcast would keep her mind off the prospect of spending time alone with Trent in his cabin. They'd stick to his kitchen and maybe his living room, depending on where they ate.

She'd be wise to stay out of his bedroom, although he might want to give her a tour and show her where he'd put the crib. Would he want it in his room when their baby was small?

Quite likely, which meant she could end up in his bedroom while they discussed that possibility. He wouldn't try to coax her into bed, though.

He'd promised this was *just dinner* and he was a man of his word... a man who affected her like no other, especially this morning when he—

Sucking in a breath, she jacked up the sound on the podcast, which only turned it into annoying background noise. A discussion of fruits and veggies couldn't compete with an image of Trent standing at the foot of her bed, arms crossed, teeth flashing in a smile as he informed her it was baby-making time.

She groaned and shut off the podcast. Besotted. Her mom had used that word to describe Trent but he wasn't the only one with that condition.

Why had she agreed to this dinner? She didn't need to see his cabin yet. That could wait. They could have discussed his parents' visit on the phone.

She'd agreed because she wanted to see him, spend time with him. Maybe she needed to prove she could do that without wanting to jump his bones.

And she was here, and in record time. In addition to ignoring the podcast she'd ignored the speedometer. The twin pines he'd mentioned were up ahead, leading her to the turnoff to his place.

Heart pounding with a mixture of anxiety and excitement, she pulled in and parked next to his dark blue truck. It dwarfed her little orange one.

Would anyone be able to see her truck from the road? Maybe it didn't matter. They'd been spotted having lunch together today, so the rumor mill would already be in motion.

Smoke curled from the chimney. She left her purse in the truck and got out, breathing in the aroma of cedar as she closed the door. A chill was in the air, even though the sun hadn't dipped behind the Sapphires yet.

A cozy fire and a homecooked meal prepared by a handsome cowboy and eaten while tucked away in the privacy of a beautiful log cabin. This would be a test, all right.

With all her senses on high alert, she started up the flagstone walk toward the porch. She would hold the line and so would he. They — wait. Someone inside the cabin just laughed. Not Trent. A woman. What the hell?

When she reached the porch, the murmur of voices drifted from inside, along with more laughter. That *was* Trent. She'd know his deep chuckle anywhere.

Then he opened the door. He wore a different shirt from the green one and the sleeves were rolled back. "Hey, there! I thought I heard a truck, but I wasn't sure."

"Mine's not very loud." She climbed the steps and crossed the porch.

"It's cute, though. Suits you. Come on in." He stepped away from the door. "Dinner's almost ready. We were hoping you'd get here soon. We're all hungry."

She speared him with a look. "Who's here? I—"

"You didn't get my text? I sent it about thirty minutes ago."

"I didn't hear it come in. I was listening to a podcast on the way." And obsessing about him. She could easily have missed the sound of an incoming text.

"It's Angie and Dallas, Brit!" Angie called from over by the fireplace. "Trent said he was making Marybeth's spaghetti sauce and we couldn't resist."

Trent lowered his voice as he met her gaze. "Thought they might help."

"Good idea." And she was disappointed that they wouldn't be alone, after all. How messed up was that?

Dallas and Angie got up from the sofa and headed toward her, Angie in the lead.

"Hey, Brit." She offered a gentle smile. "Didn't mean to startle you. Trent said he'd—"

"It's fine. I'm glad you came. But I can't figure out how you got here, though. The ranch is spread out. Nobody walks from one cabin to another."

"Except when there's a shortcut." Dallas shared a glance with Angie. "Last year when I lived in this cabin, I figured out that if I cut through the woods instead of going on the road, I'd be at Angie's back door in no time." He grinned. "And nobody was the wiser."

Brit eyed the newlyweds. "You had to sneak around to see each other? I didn't hear about that."

"Some of Angie's brothers weren't keen on me getting involved with their little sis."

"So we pulled a gotcha," Angie said. "We carried on right under their noses. It was fun."

Dallas rolled his eyes. "You had fun. I was a nervous wreck."

"In other words, you two are no strangers to intrigue and complicated situations." Brit glanced up at Trent. "Have you told them?"

"Not yet. I wanted to check with you."

"My mom says we're nuts to tell anyone but her. She said without evidence, no one will believe us."

"But if we don't tell them—"

"I know. But what if they—"

"Hey. People." Angie propped her hands on her hips. "Did aliens land a spaceship on Brit's roof? Did Elvis knock on her front door? You can't have a back-and-forth like that and not deliver the goods."

Brit agreed, but she needed Trent's okay. He gave a short nod, and she turned back to Angie, the one she felt most comfortable making eye-contact with. "This may sound wacky, but we're convinced that this morning we created a baby. As far as we're concerned, I'm pregnant."

<u>19</u>

His Brittany had guts. Not that she was *his*, Trent reminded himself. He needed to avoid that kind of possessive thinking. But he admired the way she'd owned that outrageous statement and risked being laughed at.

Dallas looked like he was fighting the urge. Trent's fist curled. Punching his brother for laughing at Brittany wouldn't be his first choice, but it was on the list.

Angie glanced at her beloved and elbowed him in the ribs. "Stop it. That's not wacky at all." She turned to Brittany. "Your mom's right. Most people would think you're imagining things and dismiss what you just said. But most people don't have Desiree McLintock for a mother."

"Your mom experienced the same thing?" She sounded like she'd unearthed the holy grail.

"Absolutely. She knew the very moment she got pregnant with me. She told me that a few months ago. She also said that wasn't the only time. She felt it with the twins, and with Rance. She's a total believer that sometimes you just know it happened."

"So I'm not crazy?"

Angie smiled and shook her head. "No, just pregnant, and to hear her talk, some days you feel pregnant *and* crazy. She says it's a trip, but a fun one. She's a pregnancy pro. You should talk to her."

Just the kind of suggestion Trent had been hoping for. "That makes a lot of sense."

"Except not now," Brittany said. "With the wedding in three days, I'll wait until after that."

"Yes, but they're leaving on their honeymoon the next day," Angie said. "And since you're looking for support and she's a logical one to give it in this situation, I hate for you to go another three weeks without talking to her."

"But I'm sure she's very busy."

"Not so much. She gave the family instructions and we're all doing the prep. Kendall, Cheyenne, Dallas and I finished up a combo bandstand and dance floor today. We had to send her off to have lunch with Andy because she kept trying to pitch in."

"Okay... then maybe... but we're so close to this event and she knows a lot of people. I, um, wouldn't want this news to get out when the entire town will be gathering for—"

"Ah, I see." Angie gazed at her. "I promise you don't have a thing to worry about. Nobody in the known universe can keep a secret better than my mother."

Dallas nodded. "That's for damned sure."

Trent peered at him. The conviction in his brother's voice and the slight tension in Angie's expression put him on alert. What sort of secret was Desiree keeping that Dallas and Angie knew and he didn't? He'd find a time to ask about it.

But this was not that time. "Let's get dinner on the table. Then we can hash a few things out while we eat."

"I'm for that, bro." Dallas gave him a thumbs up. "We'll all bring more intelligence to the subject after we get some food into us."

Angie lifted her eyebrows.

"Or I should say *I'll* be more intelligent." He winked at her. "I don't speak for my brilliant partner."

She laughed. "Now you're getting smart."

"The food's ready to be dished and brought in." The day after Trent had moved into the cabin, he'd enlisted Dallas's help to carry the large kitchen table to the living room. Then he could eat and work on his laptop in view of Cheyenne's floor-to-ceiling stone fireplace. "And the fire could use some love."

"My department." Dallas made a beeline for the hearth. "I am a professional."

Angie groaned. "You'll be sorry you let him be in charge of it. He's such a stickler."

"I'm aware. I've known him longer than you. But with Dallas around, you never have to worry about stray sparks or chimney fires."

"Yeah, I'll give him that." She blew her husband a kiss. "Love you, honeybunch."

A pang of envy caught Trent square in the chest. He'd once believed he and Cheryl had that kind of relationship. He wanted Dallas and Angie to grow old together. Maybe they'd be lucky and savvy enough to make that happen.

Angie followed him into the kitchen and opened the fridge. "Whoa, somebody stocked up on non-alcoholic beer. Want some, Brit?"

"Sounds great."

"Trent, I'll handle drinks. I know what Dallas wants. How about you?"

He couldn't give her the answer that popped into his head. "I'll take the unleaded beer, too."

"Aw that's sweet. Beau and Marsh are doing the same for Ella and Jess. It's nice." She grabbed two bottles of virgin beer from the door. "Dallas and I are drinking the leaded stuff. That bandstand project was a booger." She took out two bottles from a different shelf and headed for the living room.

Brittany scanned the kitchen. "Beautiful cabinets."

"They're impressive." He drained the pasta and began dividing it among the bowls lined up on the counter. "Especially when you know that a water leak ruined some of the bottom ones and Clint built new ones to match."

"Wow. He's talented." Her casual tone sounded breathy. "So... what can I do?"

Once again, he couldn't give an honest answer. He wanted her to kiss him until neither of them could breathe. But he wasn't supposed to be thinking that, let alone saying it out loud.

"How about taking in the salad?" He tilted his head toward a big wooden bowl. "I put in several different kinds of lettuce. I looked it up, and—"

"Leafy greens." She gave him a smile. "They're good for me and the baby. Thanks."

"You're welcome." He couldn't have the kiss, but he'd take the smile and be grateful she was here at all. He'd been surprised when she'd agreed to come and now he never wanted her to leave.

Inviting Dallas and Angie had been the right move, though. He hadn't come up with it until around four this afternoon, when his craving for her presence had threatened to undermine all his good intentions.

He'd called Dallas, and luckily his brother and sister-in-law had just finished the bandstand project and were headed home, exhausted and thrilled to have someone fix them dinner.

When Dallas had heard Brittany was coming, he'd agreed a discussion was in order. They had to get their stories straight before they picked up their parents in Missoula tomorrow afternoon.

But when Trent slid into his seat next to the woman he'd been thinking about all day, his breath caught and he lost focus. The table was round, so seating the four of them in a semi-circle meant everyone had a view of the fire, and bonus, he'd be close to Brittany.

Tactical mistake. The scent of her hair made him dizzy. His arm brushed hers and their thighs touched before she moved away. The heat of her body drew him like a moth to flame. Last time he'd been this close, they'd been naked.

"I just thought of something," Angie said.

Yeah, so had he and it was giving him a woody.

Angie gave no indication she'd picked up on his issues. "Your parents arrive tomorrow," she said. "Once you deposit them at the ranch house, there goes Brit's chance for a private talk with my mom." She turned to her. "You need to go see her in the morning."

"Can't. I'm booked solid with patient appointments."

"Okay, then tonight."

"Tonight?" Her voice squeaked. "But—"

"It's okay." Angie shifted in her seat and pulled out her phone. "She'll want to talk with you. If she finds out after the fact that I didn't contact her about this, she'll be ticked."

"She and Andy are probably fixing dinner right now. I don't want to—"

"I'll ask if we can come after dinner. Don't worry. I'll go with you. It'll be fine."

Dallas frowned. "Shouldn't Trent go with her instead of you? He's the one who helped create this m—uh, blessed event."

"This is a girls talk situation, hon. You can stay here and keep your brother company."

Trent let out a sigh of relief. He would go if Brittany wanted him there, but he'd already dealt with her mother at lunch. He'd need to bulk up before taking on the most powerful woman in Wagon Train.

20

Her finger poised over the phone, Angie turned to Brit. "Are you okay with this plan?"

Her throat felt like she'd swallowed a brick. She wanted to talk to Desiree. Really she did, but not right *now*. She'd figured on having time to work up to it, plan what she intended to say, even make some notes.

But there was no getting around it. She needed advice on navigating a single-woman pregnancy ASAP. Desiree was the most qualified person in town, maybe in the state or even the country, to give that advice.

Her upcoming marriage and honeymoon would put her out of reach for at least three weeks and by then…. yeah, it was now or never. Brit nodded. "If she's willing to see me tonight, I need to go for it."

"Alrighty." Angie made the call and her mother suggested they come over in an hour. Angie disconnected. "See? I knew she'd make the time."

"That's very generous of her." Except it left her staring at her bowl of spaghetti sprinkled with freshly grated parmesan and the ginormous helping of salad she'd dished for herself. She literally didn't have the stomach for any of it.

Trent glanced over at her. "Problem?"

"I hate to say it, but I'm too nervous to eat."

"Aww." Angie put an arm around her shoulders. "I'm sorry. I didn't think this through." She glanced over at Trent. "I didn't mean to screw up dinner."

"The rest of you go ahead." Needing to move and release her tension, Brit pushed back her chair. "I'll just—"

"No worries." Trent got up. "You and I can have leftover spaghetti after you come back." He took both bowls and headed for the kitchen. "I'll mix the pasta and sauce together and stick it in the fridge."

"I feel like a jerk after all the work you went through, Trent." Angie left her chair, too. "But we should do the same with our meal."

"Yeah, absolutely. We can eat later." Dallas didn't sound happy about it, but he followed her lead and stood. "We're not going to sit here eating if you two—"

"You absolutely should," Brit said. "I'll bet you're starving after working on that bandstand all day."

"Dallas told me that on the phone," Trent called from the kitchen. "Stay there and eat your dinner. You put in a long day."

"But if you're not eating," Dallas shot back, "that'll be weird."

"Brittany and I will go sit on the porch."

Angie glanced at her. "Did he just call you Brittany?"

"Oh, yeah," Dallas said. 'I forgot to tell you he calls her that."

Angie's brow puckered. "Why?"

"Because it sounds prettier." Trent came in and picked up their salad bowls. "I'll stick these in the fridge, too."

"I agree it's prettier. I've just never heard you called that and I was startled. I assume it's the name on your birth certificate?"

"Yep."

"How do you feel about him calling you that?"

Warmth rushed to her cheeks, since the first time he used it they'd been in bed. "I like it. It seemed strange at first, but it does have a nice ring to it. Softer. My mom called me Brittany when I was little, but once I got to school I became Brit and now she uses that, too."

Angie nodded. "Mom called me Angelique, even after I got a nickname. I asked her to stop because when you're a kid you don't want something that's so different. Now I wouldn't care."

"Do you want me to call you Angelique?" Dallas sent her a questioning glance. "It's kinda cool."

"Maybe. Let me think about it."

"Think about it while you're eating." Trent returned from the kitchen. "Please sit down and enjoy the meal and the fire. I wouldn't mind having a chance to talk to Brittany before you head over there."

He wanted a private conversation? She couldn't imagine why. Well, she could, but she thought he'd invited chaperones to avoid tempting situations.

"Okay, if you insist." Angie returned to her seat.

"Thanks, bro." Dallas sat, too. "I'll admit I'm really hungry."

"Enjoy. We'll be out on the porch if you need us." Trent picked up a knit afghan from the back of the sofa and handed it to her. "It's getting chilly."

"Thanks." As she took the soft blanket, she caught Angie and Dallas exchanging a look. Chances were they'd start talking about her relationship with Trent the minute the front door closed.

She'd be talking about it with Trent, too, once they made it out to the porch. He was acting way more like a lover than a friend. And she was enjoying it far too much.

He opened the door and ushered her out into the cool evening. The sun had dipped behind the mountains and the clouds drifted in the pale sky like shredded cotton candy.

She let out a sigh of pleasure. "This is gorgeous."

"My favorite time of day."

"Mine, too." The fresh air and scenic view calmed her.

"Table or swing?"

A table and four chairs took up the space on the left side and a brown wicker swing hung on the right. "All things considered, I should choose the table, but I'm a sucker for a porch swing."

"Then go ahead. I was planning to stand, anyway."

"That's silly. You told them we'd sit on the porch." Wrapping the afghan around her shoulders, she took a position on the swing that would give him plenty of room without having to be right next to her. She patted the green cushion. "Sit."

"Yes, ma'am." He faced her and propped his hips on the porch railing.

"I meant on the swing. Now you can't see the view."

"I have the view I want."

Her heart fluttered as she basked in the warmth in his brown eyes. Being alone with him felt good. Too good.

"I probably wasn't supposed to say that."

"And I'm not supposed to like that you did." Damn, he looked gorgeous propped against the railing, his broad shoulders slightly hunched as he gripped the railing with his strong, talented fingers. "What are we going to do about this?"

"This?"

"My mom said we give off sparks like the Fourth of July. Angie and Dallas are probably discussing that very topic right now."

"I'm sure they are. And the short answer is, I don't know what we should do in the long term. For the time being, I'm sitting on this railing instead of snuggling with you on the swing. I'm resisting the urge to haul you into my arms and kiss the living daylights out of you."

The flutter in her chest turned into a rapid drumbeat. "I didn't anticipate I'd react this way. I've had sexual relationships before. They were manageable. I never felt like…." She waved a hand in the air. "Like this."

"Like you were going to combust any second?"

"*Yes.* And that needs to change. If we're going to parent this baby as friends and not lovers, we have to be able to occupy the same room without being tempted to sneak into the nearest closet and rip off our clothes."

He sucked in a breath and looked away. "Thanks for burning that image into my brain. Now wherever we are I'll be scoping out every available closet."

"It's not a joke!"

He met her gaze. "I'm not kidding. If there was a closet on this porch—"

"Trent."

"See, that's one of the reasons we give off sparks. We've ditched the condom requirement, so we can do it on the spur of the moment anywhere we choose because we don't need anything but each other. My body vividly remembers being connected with yours and wants more of that. I'm doing my best to control that urge but it's not easy."

She gulped.

"You want it, too. I can tell. But instead we've chosen to make this a platonic friendship because it'll be in the best interests of our baby."

"Which, for the record, I still believe."

"And I support you in that, despite the missteps I've made so far."

"Like what?"

"I shouldn't have put our chairs so close together tonight."

"But you invited Angie and Dallas, which was a good thing. It also meant we had to sit closer so everyone could see the fire."

"I'm glad I invited them."

"So am I, even though I had a moment when I wished you hadn't."

He groaned. "Which means you might have considered—"

"No! I want to believe I would have just enjoyed your company and then driven home."

"I want to believe that's the way it would have gone, too." He was quiet for a moment. "I guess Desiree didn't have this problem."

"What makes you say that?"

"All the guys left. If they'd felt about Desiree the way I feel about you, they would have stuck around."

"Some did, according to my mom. At least for a few months."

"Oh? Even after she was pregnant?"

"I got that impression."

"But in the end, everyone did leave. Why?"

"Turns out either they weren't into parenthood, which might be the reason she picked them in the first place since she wanted custody, or they proposed and she rejected them."

He rubbed the back of his neck and studied the porch floor for a few seconds. Then he glanced up, his expression bleak. "Whereas I'm totally into parenthood and I have no intention of proposing. Or leaving town."

"I knew that when I asked you. I didn't think it would be a problem."

"You also didn't think we'd have enough chemistry to set fire to our neat little plan."

"I didn't figure on that at all."

He braced himself as if for a blow. "Maybe you picked the wrong guy."

_21_

The flicker of doubt in Brittany's blue eyes gave Trent a sick feeling in the pit of his stomach. "_Did_ you pick the wrong guy? Is that what you're thinking?"

"No. I picked the right guy. I wouldn't want someone who'd give up custody because he has no interest in being a parent. You were unhappy about losing that dream. That's one of the reasons I asked you to do this."

"Do you wish we weren't so attracted to each other?"

"Yes! Except not really, because I wouldn't give up that experience of creating our baby for anything."

"Then you don't regret choosing me?"

"Not for a second."

A weight lifted off his chest. "Good. Despite my whining, I don't regret saying yes. I'm excited about our daughter. I stopped at the Baby Barn this afternoon after lunch."

"And?"

"I bought a teddy bear. I know it's a cliché, but it's also an Armstrong family tradition. The minute Mom was pregnant, Dad went out and bought a teddy bear."

"That's adorable. So where is this teddy bear you bought?"

"In my bedroom closet." He grinned. "Remind me to show it to you."

"You're bad."

"Hey, you started the closet fantasy. I had nothing to do with that. Besides, I wasn't about to leave it out with Angie and Dallas here. Especially Dallas. He already thinks I'm insane."

"How about Angie?" She gave a slight push with her foot and the swing began gently moving back and forth. "Does she disapprove?"

"I think she's reserving judgment." He liked seeing her in that swing. He'd only had it up a week.

"That's what I'm getting, too. If she had major objections, you'd have heard them by now. I'm glad she's going with me over to her mom's."

"I would've gone if you'd needed me to."

"I know." She gave the swing another nudge. "You're very brave."

He chuckled. "Not really. I'm glad Angie nixed the idea of me going. I was sitting there hoping I wouldn't have to gear up for it."

"Which reminds me. When you suggested coming out on the porch, you told Angie and Dallas you wanted to talk to me before I left to see Desiree. What did you mean?"

"Nothing. It was just an excuse to get you alone and test myself. Or I should say semi-alone. I'm not going to pounce on you when they're on the other side of that door."

"But you would if they weren't here?" She dragged her foot, slowing the swing's motion.

"No." He kept eye contact as he tried to gauge her ever-shifting mood. "Well, I say that, but I'd have a tough time resisting the urge if you had your pounce-on-me expression on your face."

"I have an expression like that?"

"Uh-huh. That's exactly how you looked at me this morning." A moment that would live forever in his heart.

And now the flicker of doubt was back in her eyes.

He took a deep breath. Might as well find out where it came from. "But it's not how you're looking at me now. What's wrong? You said you don't regret choosing me, but you're upset. Is it this pesky attraction situation? We'll deal with it. We'll—"

"You're suffering." She held the swing stationary. "I hate that."

"Suffering? No. Frustrated? Sure, but I'm not—"

"I call it suffering. I invited you into my bed and you had a great time, and then—"

"*We* had a great time."

"Okay, *we* did. But I'm talking about you right now. You had every right to believe this project would last at least several days. I think I even mentioned this week was my fertile time."

"You did." And he had figured on a longer time span.

"Yet only hours after we started, we're done."

"Mostly because of my oversized ego. You dreamed I was a knight on a horse and that played right into my need to be your hero."

"You *were* my hero. And your reward is constant frustration, aka suffering. What's good about that?"

"My reward is taking satisfaction in a job well done. We made a baby girl. That was our goal and we accomplished it."

"But then what? Your engines were running full out and then we abruptly ended the operation."

"It's what we agreed to. What *I* agreed to." Then the light dawned. He might want to shut the heck up and listen to the subtext of her argument. He wasn't the only frustrated person on this porch.

"I admire you for sticking with the plan even when it didn't work out the way you expected. That shows character."

"Thank you." Was she talking herself into a renegotiation? One he'd be very happy about? His body began to hum.

"I still believe we should avoid a romantic relationship."

But was something else still on the table? He cleared the sudden attack of lust from his throat. "As I told your mom, I don't believe in romance anymore." Her mom hadn't liked hearing that, but Brittany had given him a subtle thumbs up for that comment.

"I'm not sure I ever did believe in it. Maybe when I was younger, when I was into fairy princesses, but by the time I was ten or so, I was over it."

"Took me a little longer."

"But the scales have fallen from your eyes?"

"Scales, rose petals, whatever was blocking my view."

"And these sparks my mom's referring to, they have nothing to do with romance, right?"

"Nothing whatsoever." He liked where this discussion was going. So did his randy body.

"Even though we've used the term *making love* instead of *having sex*?"

"I understand what you're saying. The thing is, when we decided to create this baby, we didn't just *have sex*. It was more meaningful than that." And the video of their last encounter was rolling in his head.

"I agree."

"But I wouldn't call it romantic, either. It was more... elemental." The possibility of an alternate ending to the evening sent heat to his groin and emptied his lungs.

"Elemental. I like that description."

Her low, sensual murmur didn't help his condition. The light was low out here. He had trouble reading her expression to gauge her mood. But it wasn't that low, and any second now she'd know exactly what he was thinking.

He pushed away from the railing. "But it was more than that." Walking toward the steps, he gripped the nearest post and kept his back to her. "And it seems I've failed this test. I want you so much right now I can't see straight."

"That's what I mean. You're suffering."

"But you're not?"

"If I am, it's my own fault. I'm the one who got us into this. You would have been content with a one-night stand."

He snorted. "Content isn't the word I would have chosen. That lollapalooza of a kiss in the truck gave me a hint I'd get more than I'd bargained for. I knew I'd be asking for an extension on our one-night agreement."

"I had the exact same thought. My body was shouting *Hallelujah. Let the games begin.*"

He chuckled. "Yeah. I could tell."

She fell silent for a moment. "So here we are."

"Here we are." Thanks to the rapidly dropping temperature, he'd had some success cooling off his equipment, but he decided to keep his back to her in case she was about to say something that would start the process all over again.

"I think it's time to face facts."

"Which ones?"

"The most obvious and immediate. This red-hot—"

The sound of knocking ended whatever she was about to say. He turned, thinking she'd made that noise, but no, someone was knocking on the door from the *inside.* What the hell?

The door opened a crack. "Everybody decent?"

It was Angie giving them a courtesy knock.

Brittany laughed. "Of course we're decent. It's cold out here."

"That never stopped me." She poked her head out. "We finished eating and we — hey, are you two arguing?"

"Not at all." He managed to sound normal. "Just discussing something." And she'd interrupted at a critical moment.

Maybe just as well. Whatever was going on with Brittany, she wasn't totally committed one way or the other. Her comment that they had to face facts was prefaced by *I think*.

Did he want her to change her mind about how they'd conduct this relationship? His body shouted *yes* but his cautious heart had reservations. That said, if she invited him back into her bed, he'd jump at the chance. And deal with the fallout later.

22

Although Brit had driven to the ranch house at night before, she gratefully accepted Angie's offer to give her directions. Tall trees and zero streetlights created deep shadows. Combine that with a severe case of nerves, and she'd be lost without Angie as her co-pilot.

"I appreciate you setting this up." She slowed when her headlights revealed a deep rut. "I wish I'd thought about talking to your mom a long time ago."

"At least you're doing it now."

"Yeah, but I've approached this concept ass backwards. I'm seeking her advice after the fact."

"Blame it on your birthday. She'll understand. I've had my share of birthday snafus."

"I'd love to say that was the reason, except shouldn't I have wigged out at thirty instead of thirty-one?"

"No, because I'll bet you were prepared for thirty. Everybody says that's the biggie. Then you let down your guard and thirty-one grabbed you by the short hairs."

"There's some truth to that. Plus Ella's pregnancy affected my state of mind."

"And Trent. Don't forget you were unexpectedly presented with a tasty option. Those Armstrong brothers have it going on."

"Don't I know it. How soon is the turnoff?"

"Not far, but take it slow and watch for critters. This time of year they act like daredevils flirting with death. It's like they think it's a contest."

"I'll go super slow. Also, before we get there, I need to know what's appropriate to ask and what isn't."

"That's easy. You can ask her about anything that happened in the past, including how she handled her affairs with the dads. But her sexual relationship with Andy is off-limits."

"I should hope so! Good grief. I would never—"

"I didn't think you'd go there. No reason to. He's not one of the dads. I think of him as Super Dad, the only man who got Mom to say yes. That puts him in a whole other category."

"It's impressive that he accomplished that."

"No kidding. And she adores him. As far as she's concerned, Andy Hartmann hung the moon and put every star in its place. She protects their privacy with breathtaking ferocity. And I love that she does."

"I'm assuming he won't take part in the discussion." She put on the brakes as something small and furry ran across the road.

"Not a chance. He'll be tucked away in their suite with a good book. But they don't keep secrets from each other. He'll have access to anything you tell her, but chances are he won't ask. He's good that way. Respectful of delicate situations."

"You think a lot of him."

"Yes, ma'am. We all love him to bits. We didn't know what we were missing until Andy became a part of our lives. Now we can't imagine not having him around. Although I'm thrilled they're taking this fabulous honeymoon, it'll feel very strange having them gone for two weeks."

"Are you sure I'm not interrupting? They must have packing to do. Two weeks is a long time."

"They did that last weekend. Two medium-sized duffels is all they'll take. And backpacks."

"Duffels and backpacks? Where are they going?"

"Kenya."

"Wow! I didn't hear that. A safari?"

"Not exactly. They'll be out in the African bush visiting the Sheldrick Wildlife Trust. It rescues orphaned elephants and eventually reintroduces them into the wild."

"Sounds amazing."

"They're both so excited. Okay, slow down. It's the next road on your left."

Brit's headlights flashed on a small wooden sign that read D. McLintock. "I never noticed that sign before. It'd be easy to miss."

"That's fine with her. She doesn't encourage looky-loos."

"But won't most of the town be out here on Saturday for the reception?"

"Wagon Trainers are fine. People in town are respectful of her privacy. It's the tourists she doesn't want wandering around out here."

"Makes sense. It is a beautiful spot, and...whoa! Did you guys add a bunch of lights to the house and the trees?" She stopped the truck and stared at the fairyland that had appeared as she'd rounded a curve in the road.

Angie laughed. "A whole lotta lights. And we lit the bandstand and dance floor, too."

"I see that. Gorgeous." The trees surrounding the house always had some fairy lights, but that number had tripled.

The bandstand sitting in the front yard had its share of fairy lights. It was also festooned with at least a dozen strands of multicolored lanterns of the same design as the white ones she'd strung on her fourposter. The front porch had some, too.

Brit eased up on the brake and drove toward a large parking space currently occupied only by Desiree's purple F-350 and Andy's modest white truck with *Wagon Train Sentinel* stenciled on the door panel. "Congrats to the construction crew. The place looks like a Hollywood set."

"I know, right? I actually meant to turn off a few of the lights before we left, but the sun was still up and I forgot. I like seeing the effect, though. And at least they're LEDs."

"I was at the Buffalo today and saw the sign that they're closing on Saturday. Seeing this display, I get it. Who wants to be at the Buffalo when they could be here? There's no reason to stay open for a few stray tourists."

"There won't be many of those, either. The hotel blocked out Saturday night and so did Mrs. J so she didn't have to host anybody at the B&B. This is the event of the year, maybe the decade."

"Maybe the century! I can't believe your mother is taking time for me right now. That's crazy."

"Like I said, we let her draw up the plans, but we're executing them. We might even be more excited than she is. It's a big deal for all of us."

"I'm happy for you guys. And for them."

Weddings had become commonplace for the McLintocks recently, and they were always fun. Brit had enjoyed herself at each one, and this celebration would be the granddaddy of them all.

Did she get a twinge of longing when she was surrounded by such an abundance of light and color? Sure. This was what her ten-year-old self had dreamed her wedding day would be like.

Then she'd grown up.

23

Dallas helped Trent load the dishwasher and then motioned toward the fridge. "Mind if I have another beer?"

"By all means."

"Want one?"

"I still have the one from dinner."

"It'll be flat by now. You could have a real beer. She's not here."

"Considering the mood I'm in, I wouldn't stop with one and I want to be sober when she gets back."

"Suit yourself. Which one is yours? There's two in here with the cap mashed back on. Which never works, by the way. You need those little silicone stoppers."

"I never saw the point. I don't drink half a beer and save the rest."

"Me, either. You put these in here, is yours on the right or the left?"

"I don't remember. Just pick one."

Dallas gave him a look. "That was fast."

"What?"

"Sharing each other's spit." He grabbed one of the opened beers, closed the fridge door with his shoulder and nudged the cap into the trash can with his thumb. "Four days ago you barely knew who she was." He handed over the beer.

"A lot can happen in four days." He led the way back into the living room.

"Apparently."

"Thanks for keeping track of the fire." Trent flopped down on the sofa. The fire crackled and popped, two fresh logs perched on top of the three already engulfed in flames.

"It's what I do." His brother sprawled at the other end. "Okay, the truth, bro. Do you *really* believe she's pregnant?"

"Yes." He took a long swallow of the beer, which was, as Dallas had predicted, flat. He grimaced and took another swallow.

"Look at me and tell me you believe she's PG."

He grinned. How many times had his big brother confronted him like this over the years? Hundreds. He'd convinced himself he could tell when Trent was pulling a fast one. Sometimes he could. Mostly he couldn't. "Think I'm lying?"

"More likely stretching the truth. It's always possible she is, and she's dead certain of it, so you're willing to go along. At least, that's my theory."

"Good theory." Trent shifted his position and stared directly at Dallas. "She's pregnant, bro. It's the perfect time according to her cycle and guys are more potent in the morning, so logically we had an excellent chance of success."

"Then why not go with *possibly* instead of declaring it's a done deal?"

"Because I felt it happen."

He rolled his eyes. "Sure you did." He took a swig of his beer.

"This is none of my business, but since we're on the subject, are you and Angie trying?"

"Why do you ask?"

"Because based on that eye roll, I don't think you are."

"Okay, we're not, smartass. Not yet, anyway. What's your point?"

"Once you ditch the condoms, you'll know what I'm talking about. What you're experiencing now may seem great, but it's like holding hands with a work glove on."

Dallas's eyes went wide. "Well, thanks for that. Now I'm jealous as hell. And ready to get into the game."

"Why don't you?"

"Economics. We want to make sure Handywomen continues to run smoothly. Angie's in no hurry to have a baby and as Jodie gets older, Kendall can take on more duties. When the time comes, Cheyenne and I will stop working the same shift so we can trade off childcare."

"That makes a lot of sense. It sure would lighten the load for Angie and Kendall. I'm surprised you haven't done it already."

"We haven't because we enjoy working together and Angie says there's no rush. But after your work glove comment I'm thinking I'd rather skip the pleasure of working with Cheyenne and start making babies."

"I'm telling you, bro, it'll change your life. You won't want to go back."

"That good, huh?"

"That good."

"No wonder you can't take your eyes off her. Do I understand correctly that the two of you are supposed to shift gears and just be buddies, now?"

"That's the way she had it figured from the beginning. Once we made a kid, that part of the relationship ended."

"Where'd she get that nutty idea?"

"She thought that's the way Desiree had worked her program. Turns out she was wrong. Her mom told her Desiree had a passionate affair with each of those guys."

"That's what you talked about on the porch?"

"Yep." He drained the bottle.

"Will she change her mind, then?"

"Maybe. Maybe not. Angie poked her head out right when we'd made it to that critical point in the conversation."

"Bet you loved that interruption."

"Actually, I'm glad she did it. Gives me a chance to think when I'm not swimming in testosterone."

"What's there to think about? You just convinced me it's the best time a guy could ever hope for."

"Which is great for someone like you, but not so great for someone like me."

"You mean someone who will never in this lifetime walk down the aisle again?"

"Exactly."

"Want my opinion?"

He smiled. "Do I have a choice?"

"Not really. I'm your big brother and giving advice is in my job description." He pushed himself off the sofa. "First I need another beer." He grabbed Trent's empty. "Want me to bring you that other flat one?"

"Sure. I don't want her to have to drink it."

"I'm so glad you said that. It supports what I'm about to suggest." He glanced at the fire. "You might want to throw on another log."

"I thought you were in charge of that."

"I am, but I have enough to do with fetching beer and delivering pearls of wisdom. I'm delegating the job to you."

Trent put two logs on the fire instead of one. No telling how soon Angie and Brittany would be back and he wanted it going while he served the warmed up meal.

For some reason Dallas had mellowed toward a concept he'd soundly rejected yesterday morning. Only yesterday? His emotions had been on a wild ride since then, and it wasn't over yet.

He replaced the fireplace screen.

"Here's your other flat beer." Dallas came in and handed it to him. "I considered pouring it out and getting you a good one, but I didn't."

"Thanks. It's fine." He took a sip to prove it.

"How'd Brit like the swing?"

He blinked. "What about the advice?"

"I'm getting to it. Did she sit on the swing?"

"She did. She liked it, likes swings in general. Thanks for helping me hang it last week."

"You're welcome. Why'd you buy it?"

"Because I like swings. Why in God's name are we discussing them?"

"Because a single guy who never intends to settle down with a woman has very little reason to buy one. How many times since you bought it have you sat in it?"

"None, but I've been busy. I—"

"Do you really think you're going to sit out there by your lonesome, swinging away? Can you picture that?"

"I could take a nap on it."

"Have you tried stretching out on that thing? There's no way you could get comfortable enough to take a nap."

"So I bought it because it looks nice. A wicker swing looks good on a porch. Can we move on?"

"Absolutely, right after I make my point that it's a cozy couples swing, perfect for cuddling with someone you care about."

"So what?"

"So you say you're finished with romance, reject the myth of happily ever after, but you buy that swing. I call bullshit."

"It's just a swing, dammit!"

"It's evidence. And I have more. You're knocking yourself out to please Brit. You bought her unleaded beer, made a big salad, leaped to handle the situation when she couldn't eat and volunteered to keep her company with warmed up spaghetti. Oh, and you grabbed a blanket so she wouldn't catch a chill."

"Mom and Dad taught us to—"

"Be considerate? Buddy, you're way past considerate. You're in laying your coat over a mud puddle territory. And you're loving it. Don't tell me you don't enjoy taking care of her because it's clear you do."

Trent stared at him, speechless. Finally he came up with a plausible reason for his behavior. "She's pregnant with my kid. Our kid."

"That's not it. I recognize what I'm seeing, bro. I do stuff like that for Angie all the time and she's not pregnant. I do it because I'm crazy about her and it's fun to think of ways to make her happy and more comfortable. She does the same for me."

He glanced away and focused on the flames dancing behind the screen. "You're right. It is fun. For the first couple of years, I loved being married to Cheryl. But then—"

"She was a con artist, bro. No substance. She was good at faking it, though. None of us saw through her until it was too late."

"Least of all me. And thanks to her, weddings are my worst nightmare."

"Even mine?"

Trent met his gaze. "Especially yours. I didn't know Angie. You could have been headed for the same kind of misery I'd dealt with."

"You hid it well."

"Had to. You were counting on me."

"And now?"

"I'm cautiously optimistic."

"Why?"

"Because of this family. They're like ours, only bigger. They treat each other well."

"You do remember what I told you we went through with her brothers, right?"

"Of course I remember. And Angie handled it in a very classy way. That story was what convinced me she's not likely to stab you in the back."

"I can safely say she's not. And for what it's worth, neither is Brit."

He nodded in agreement. "If I thought she would, I'd never have agreed to the baby plan." He took another swallow of the beer. "This really tastes terrible when it goes flat."

"But you'll drink it because you don't want Brit drinking it or feeling guilty because it went down the drain. And you won't pour it down the drain because you're not willing to lie to her, even about something small."

"That about sums it up." He guzzled the rest and glanced at his brother. "Was there some advice buried in that long, drawn-out commentary? Because if there was, I missed it."

"No, but here it comes. It took a lot of cojones for Brit to consider this plan. She's a gutsy lady."

"You're not telling me anything I don't know."

"I'm married to a gutsy lady and here's the first piece of advice. She won't admire you if you let her be in charge all the time. Take the reins once in a while."

He nodded. He'd done that this morning, with spectacular results. "That's good advice."

"I don't know what to tell you about this platonic friendship agreement you made with her. What were you thinking?"

Trent opened his mouth.

"Never mind. You were temporarily insane. But judging from what I've seen tonight, that plan is on its way out. If it is, just go with it."

"I don't know what *it* is."

"From where I stand, bro, it looks a lot like a second chance. Now go get some cards. I'll let you beat me at gin rummy."

24

Desiree and her collie Sam greeted them at the door. As Angie had predicted, Andy was nowhere in sight.

Desiree led them back to the living room where the fire was burning brightly and a tray sat on the coffee table. Just tea. No snacks. Sam surveyed the tray as if to confirm that before trotting over to his bed by the fire and flopping down.

"I made herbal tea, Brit," she said. "It'll settle your stomach."

"How'd you know it needs settling?"

"Because Angie said you had an issue that I was uniquely qualified to help you with. Since you're of child-bearing age, that's likely the heart of the matter. And upset tummies are a given in those situations."

"Good deduction."

Reaching for a pot of honey with three sticks protruding from the top, Desiree handed it to her. "Twirl one of those little sticks around and the grooved spool at the end will gather up the honey. Put it in your cup and then I'll pour the tea. Honey's soothing, too."

"Thank you. I feel better already." It wasn't exactly true, but she wanted it to be. Desiree was so kind to see her tonight, when surely she'd rather be hanging out with Andy.

After everyone had their honey-laced tea, Desiree took a seat in the armchair to the right of the sofa. Motioning to the sofa, Angie sat down and Brit settled in beside her.

"Sam and I went for a walk before you came." Desiree beamed at Angie. "What a spectacular job on the bandstand and dance floor!"

"It looks amazing." Brit cradled the tea on her lap. "I was dazzled when we drove in."

"It looks good, if I do say so myself." Taking a sip of tea, Angie leaned back against the cushions.

Brit did not. Instead she took a gulp of tea. The warm, sweet liquid did calm her slightly.

"Sam and I walked around on it and it's solid as a rock. Will you really be able to disassemble it and put it back together for the next shindig?"

"Yes, ma'am. We made a diagram and marked everything as we went."

"Looks like we'll be having some fun parties this summer." Desiree took a sip of her tea before focusing on Brit. "Alrighty, then. Tell me what's going on."

The teacup rattled on the saucer so she set it down on the coffee table. She had flashbacks of giving reports in school as she dragged in a breath.

Sticking to the significant details, she touched on the impulsive night with Trent, the discovery that he wouldn't marry again, his disappointment at not having kids, and her suggestion they co-parent while maintaining separate lives.

She managed to get through it without hyperventilating. When she finished, her heart was pounding and her cheeks were on fire. "Angie said you would believe me when I say this next part."

"Then I probably will."

"I'm absolutely sure I got pregnant this morning."

Desiree didn't gasp or even blink. "I do believe you, although you may have set a record for efficiency in that department."

"Yes, ma'am." Which had put her in an awkward spot with Trent.

"Technically medical science doesn't consider you pregnant yet, but for all intents and purposes, you are. Who knows besides Dallas and Angie?"

"My mom. And Trent wants to tell his parents about our… arrangement. That way when it's official they won't think it was an accident. But he's not sure how much to say."

"I suggest he tell Harry and Vanessa exactly what you just told me."

"But will *they* believe it?"

Desiree smiled. "Think about it. They named their children after the city where they were conceived."

"But they could have figured that out after the fact."

"Maybe, but in every case but Trent's they went to a three-day insurance conference in that city. They emphasize that when they tell the story.

I think they'll believe you. If they don't, I'll back you up."

"Thank you." She hadn't considered that option. "I keep forgetting they'll be staying with you."

Angie gazed at her mother. "Good thinking about the naming thing. I didn't put that together." She turned to Brit. "So tell Harry and Vanessa they're going to be grandparents, but please don't promise to follow their naming tradition."

Brit surprised herself with a burst of laughter that turned into a giggle. "You don't want a niece named Wagon Train?"

"Or Conestoga, or Wheel, or Spoke, or—"

"Montana's not bad, though." Desiree's face lit up. "In fact, if you don't like it, I'll suggest it to Jess and Ella and see whether they do. It's gender neutral, and it has a decidedly Western flavor. Or you could cheat a little and go with Missoula, although Montana is—"

"Whoops, my bad, Mom."

"What?"

"I didn't mean to get you started."

"Get her started on what?"

"Naming the baby. We could spend hours on that alone."

Desiree grinned. "I admit it. I love that part. The minute I knew I was pregnant, I started the name search. Since I grew up watching old TV Westerns, that's where I went for inspiration. Except for Angie and Beau. Oh, and Sky."

"Where did you get Angelique? We were just talking about her name."

"Louis L'Amore's daughter is named that. His son's name is Beau."

"And you're a Louis L'Amore fan. That's a nice tribute. Where did Sky's name come from?"

"Skyler is the hero in M.R. Morrison's first book."

"Huh. I read it years ago, but I never made the connection with Sky. I thought maybe it came from Big Sky Country."

"When my brother was about thirteen," Angie said, "he'd go around saying *you're in Big Sky Country* and flexing his muscles. He tried to get me to call him Big Sky. I refused. He wasn't any bigger than the others."

"Now I'm gonna tease him about that."

"You should. You'll make him blush. It's cute."

"I do like the name Montana. I'll see what Trent thinks, but if you want to say something to Jess and Ella, go ahead. It was your idea."

"I'll wait. If Trent likes it, you'd have something that would make Harry and Vanessa happy. They'd never want you to saddle your kid with a name like Wagon Train. There are limits."

"You say that, Mom, but Dallas told me they almost went to a conference in Charlotte the weekend he was conceived."

"Ah, but they instinctively chose the right city. Or if they'd gone to Charlotte, they would have had a girl."

"There's a scary thought. If there'd been no Dallas I'd still be single and Trent would be living in New Jersey."

Brit instinctively touched her stomach. "I'm so glad they went to Texas."

"Me, too, girlfriend. Me, too."

Desiree finished her tea and set it on the coffee table. "If Trent wants to co-parent, does he want to share custody?"

"He does."

"That's not the way I handled it."

"I know."

Desiree gave her a long look. "I've been sitting here wondering if you got this idea from me."

Her flush returned. "Well, I... yes, to be honest, I did. Your decision to have kids without waiting for the perfect guy to come along has fascinated me for years."

"It wasn't without its own complications."

"I'm sure. But you were picky. I'm picky. I haven't met the man I want to spend a lifetime with."

"I understand completely. On the other hand, sharing custody presents some of the same problems as being married, which is why I insisted on being the sole guardian."

"I get that." Brit took a deep breath. She couldn't very well tell Desiree that she'd never choose a man who'd willingly sign away his rights. "But Trent's longing to be a father is one of the reasons I came up with the plan."

"I'm not surprised he wants children. He'll be a good dad."

"He will. And his hours are flexible while mine usually aren't. That will help as we work out a childcare schedule."

"You might not have to hire anyone, then."

"Probably not. My mom will pitch in when she can."

"So will Buck and Marybeth if you need them. They've never met a baby they didn't love. Neither have I, for that matter. I'll help when I can, although my dance card's getting filled up fast."

"Whereas my mom's is totally open, so she'll be my first line of defense. I mean, mine and Trent's."

"But you won't be living together?"

"No. It'll involve some driving, but we'll figure it out. We'll keep the lines of communication open. I think the key will be maintaining our friendship."

"I thought you didn't know each other before Saturday night."

"We didn't, but..." She flushed. "I see what you're getting at. We'll need to build that friendship."

"Which shouldn't be hard. I can tell you think he's an honorable man."

"Extremely honorable."

"And intelligent."

"Very."

"And nice to look at."

Her face heated again. "Yes."

"That was extremely important to me when I chose the fathers of my children."

"Because the baby would carry his genes?"

"Well, yes. But he needed to look good in his jeans, if you get my meaning."

"Oh."

"There'd be no baby, period, unless the man flipped all my switches. I wouldn't go to bed with a guy just to make a baby. That's... I'm not sure what it is, but it's not my speed."

"So you tested them out first?"

"You betcha. There was always a trial run with a condom. Kind of like you did on Saturday night, although you weren't thinking of it that way."

"No, but now that you say that, I'd already ticked that box. I was fantasizing about him the whole time I was at the Buffalo with Ella and Faye."

"The Buffalo served that purpose for me, too. I found three of the dads there." Desiree glanced at Angie. "Are you okay with how this discussion is going? Because if at any point you want to take Sam for a walk so you don't have to listen to your mother talk about her checkered past..."

"Oh, I'm staying. I wouldn't miss this for the world. Did you meet my dad at the Buffalo?"

"No. I hired him to build bookshelves for me. That's it. I had no agenda. But there he was every day, wearing that sexy toolbelt, and I couldn't help myself."

"Do you think you might have married him? Because the boys have said—"

"I don't know, sweetie. That's really impossible to say."

"They all liked him."

"So did I. He was a special guy. And Brit, to your point about custody, he was the only one who refused to sign those papers. And I didn't push it."

"Did he move in?"

"Yes. But I was still dead-set against marriage. I wanted complete control of my life. And he'd started hinting. If I'd refused to marry him, he might have left."

"That makes my point. If Trent and I avoid all that, if we don't live together and we don't have sex anymore, then we can just be friends and—"

"Whoa, Nellie." Desiree stared at her. "Did you cut that boy off?"

"It was a mutual decision. We've agreed not to get romantically involved."

"Correct me if I'm wrong, but didn't you start this process late last night and conclude it early this morning?"

"That's true."

"Having been told multiple times the ecstasy a man feels when he has sex without a condom, I'll assume he had a very good time."

Brit swallowed. "He did. We both did."

"And now you expect him to go cold turkey?"

"I've been worried about that. It seemed like the right call, but..."

"Is he happy about the decision?"

"He says he's fine, but I don't think he is."

"I guaran-damn-tee he's not."

"But ultimately we're shooting for a platonic friendship like you have with the fathers of your children."

"Honey, that took years."

"Maybe we're expecting too much too soon."

"You think?"

"But it's been our goal from the beginning."

"When was that, exactly?"

"I first suggested the idea around two a.m. Sunday morning. He told me yes about eleven-fifteen last night." She caught Desiree's look. "You're right. It'll take a lot more time to make the transition. But how do we get there if we keep having sex?"

Desiree let out a sigh. "That's a million-dollar question and all I can offer is my two cents worth. You and Trent will have to work this out in a way that's satisfactory to both of you. You're the only ones who can create a resolution."

"I think I knew that."

"One more thing to keep in mind."

"I'm listening."

"You'll never have a reasonable discussion with a sexually frustrated man."

25

Trent hadn't heard Brittany's truck pull up the first time, when she'd arrived for dinner, but he was hypersensitive to the sound when she came back from seeing Desiree. He tossed down his hand. "Game's over."

"Thank the Lord." Dallas gathered up the cards. "I don't think I've ever seen you play this bad. Not even when you were drunk."

"Got things on my mind." He stood. "Get the door, okay? I need to heat up the spaghetti." He started toward the kitchen.

"I have a better idea." With the agility of a former tight end, Dallas left his chair and blocked his path. "You get the door and I'll heat up the spaghetti. You've spent enough time fussing over those noodles."

Laughing, he threw himself into the game of outmaneuvering Dallas. "My kitchen, my noodles."

"I mean it, little brother." Arms out, he countered Trent's every move. "Go talk with your lady. I'm a firefighter. I can heat up leftovers."

"Hey, we're back!" Angie came through the front door with Brittany right behind her. "Are you two dancing? If you are, that's the worst line dance move I've ever seen."

Trent sighed. "So much for getting the door." He turned toward Angie. "Your husband's trying to take over my kitchen."

"I'm not just trying. I've done it. Territory secured."

"Great idea, honeybunch. I'll help. You two sit by the fire and have a chat. Dinner will be on the table in a jiffy."

Trent glanced at Brittany. "Looks like I invited a couple of bossy people into my house. Worse yet, I'm related to 'em."

"We can hear you," Angie called out. "Brit, don't you have some things you want to share with Trent?"

She smiled at him. "You're right. Extremely bossy guests."

"Let's make them happy and go sit by the fire." He let her pick a spot and then he sat down, leaving some space between them.

"Nice fire." She settled back against the cushions.

"Thanks." It needed tending, but he didn't want to be messing with the fire right now. He wanted to be looking at her face when she talked. "What did Desiree have to say?"

"First of all, that shared custody is more complicated."

"We know that." She seemed a lot calmer than she had been when she left.

"She said it had some of the drawbacks of being married, which was why she insisted on being the sole guardian." She waited, as if expecting a response.

"If you think I'll change my mind and give you that, I won't."

"It ties us together legally."

"If it does, it does. I want a voice in what goes on with our kid." And a connection to her. That realization startled him.

Her expression warmed. "I would never say this to Desiree, but I wouldn't have a child with a man who'd give up his rights."

If things were different between them, this would be the moment he'd draw her into his arms and thank her for choosing him. Kisses would be involved. "Obviously she found guys who were fine with it."

"Except for one. Angie's father refused to give her sole custody and she didn't push it."

"Huh. Good for him."

"She told Angie about it once she was old enough to understand. She's kept it to herself out of kindness to her brothers, although I'm guessing she's shared it with Dallas. On the way home she mentioned how much that little bit of information means to her."

"Sure it does. How did he die?"

"In a car accident before she was born. It's sad she never knew him, but Desiree said he'd started hinting at getting married and she was still against it. If she'd refused to marry him, he might have left."

"Or she might have said yes. Sounds like their relationship was different. He stood up to her on the joint custody issue. I don't think she respects a pushover. Andy holds his own with her."

"You'd know that better than I do, since you spend so much time with this family. By the way, she said you'll make a great dad."

"She did? That was nice of her."

"Oh, she's looking out for your interests. She thinks that ending our sexual relationship just because we made a baby in record time is cruel and unusual punishment."

His chest tightened. "She said that to you? That's pretty harsh."

"She didn't use those words. I'm paraphrasing." She took a shaky breath. "But that was the gist."

"Hey, I don't feel that way." He started to reach for her. Stopped himself.

"I know, but she has a point. It's the same one I was trying to make when we were out on the porch."

"Don't blame yourself. You didn't anticipate this situation any more than I did."

"But I should have. I didn't look before I leaped."

"I looked, and then jumped anyway. I'm still not sorry."

"Neither am I, but... it leaves us with this issue." She clasped her hands in her lap. "You almost touched me just now, but you drew back."

"It's better if I don't."

"But you wanted to."

He held her gaze. "That's only the tip of the iceberg. But I guess that's natural considering that just this morning—"

'Time for din-din!" Angie skirted an armchair that sat catty-corner to the sofa and put down a tray on the coffee table in front of Brittany.

Dallas walked around the matching one on Trent's left and placed a second tray in front of Trent. "Will there be anything else, sir?"

He glanced up at his older brother. "We're eating here?"

"Looks like it. Think you can manage without spilling on yourself?"

"I'll do my best."

"Your fire's in sad shape, dude."

"Don't tease him." Angie sat in the armchair closest to Brittany. "They've had things to discuss. Did you get everything sorted out?"

"Not quite." Brittany picked up her pasta bowl. "Thanks for doing this. I didn't think I was hungry but my stomach just told me different."

"Sorry about the noodles. They got cut up in the process, but at least that makes them easier to eat."

Dallas moved the fireplace screen. "At the firehouse we cut 'em up on purpose, but Angie won't let me do that at home."

"And I'm sticking to it. Oh, hon, before you add any log to that fire, you might want to check with your brother. We're getting close to bedtime."

Trent almost choked on his spaghetti.

"Didn't think of that." Dallas turned around, a log in each of his gloved hands. "You want me to build up the fire or leave it be?"

He managed to swallow without asphyxiating himself. "Leave it, please."

Dallas returned the logs to the wood box. "Then I'll just spread out the coals so it'll die out faster. I lost track of time. We should be getting home pretty soon, huh?"

"First we need to discuss what Desiree said about your folks. Brit, did you tell him?"

"We didn't get to that."

Dallas replaced the fireplace screen. "Well, Angie told me while we were in the kitchen, and you'll be surprised to hear, bro, that Desiree thinks we can tell the folks that Brit's pregnant and they won't bat an eye."

"Really."

"Surprised the hell out of me, too." He claimed the armchair next to Trent. "But I guess it makes sense. Tell 'em why, Angie."

"Mom thinks since they named every kid after the city where they were conceived, they could have had the same experience you two just had. And they'll have no trouble believing it."

"I hadn't thought of it that way, but it's a decent theory." He gazed at his brother. "So if I say it, you'll back me up?"

"I will. You've made a believer out of me."

"Alrighty, then. We have a game plan for the drive home."

"Just one thing. They probably won't, but on the slim chance they'll try to talk you into naming your kid Wagon Tr—"

"Holy hell. I hadn't even thought of that. It won't be happening."

"That's a relief."

He glanced at Brittany. "I have a hard time believing they'd even suggest it, but don't worry. That's a non-starter."

"I know, but how do you like Montana?"

"Montana." He let it sit in his mind for a few seconds. "I like it. Whose idea was that?"

"My mom's." Angie said. "She's the baby naming champion. You could tell your parents that's a name you're considering. That should make them happy because it honors the family tradition, even if it's the state and not the city."

"It's an awesome idea." Dallas sat forward in his chair. "But if you guys take Montana, what's left for our kid?"

"I'm way ahead of you, honeybunch." Angie gave him a smile. "We'll reverse-engineer this. We'll pick a Montana city name we like and go have sex there."

"What if I'd rather make a baby in the comfort of our own home?"

"Um, well, then I guess—"

"When you were gone, Trent and I got to talking and I'm wondering if we should rethink our baby plan, maybe move it up some."

"Move it up? To when?"

"Now."

"*Now*?"

"I mean, when we get home."

"Oh, good, because I doubt present company would appreciate being spectators at that event. Trent, did you give my husband baby fever?"

"Could be. It wasn't my goal, but—"

"No worries, dude. I'm glad we got into the subject. I have a feeling I'll be thanking you for—"

"You know what?" Angie stood. "I think it's time for us to shove off."

"I'll get our jackets." Dallas quickly left his chair and made a beeline for the coatrack near the door. "What time are you picking me up tomorrow, bro?"

"Ten should get us there in time."

"Sounds good." He helped Angie on with her jacket and shrugged into his. "See you then." He put on his hat and followed Angie toward the kitchen and the cabin's back door. "That's a cool idea you had about traveling to different cities, Angie. I just don't like the thought of a strange bed when we could have the luxury of our—"

"Then I hope you like the name Rowdy."

He laughed. "I kinda do. We've got Rowdy, bro," he called over his shoulder. "Just in case you decide to have a second one, Rowdy's taken."

The click of the back door latch sent Trent's energy level through the roof. Having his brother and sister-in-law in the cabin had lowered the temperature considerably.

But they were gone. Turning, he looked into blue eyes that sent a clear message. And he was on fire.

<u>26</u>

Brit's plan, which had looked brilliant in the early hours of her thirty-first birthday, could be totally unworkable. Desiree had implied as much.

But when Trent abandoned his meal, stood and held out his hand, she didn't give a damn. If she'd landed herself in a mess, it wasn't all bad news. She was pregnant with a baby girl, and a man who flipped all her switches, as Desiree would say, had just issued a silent invitation.

Better yet, he assumed her acceptance of his invitation. He didn't hesitate or question. He simply led her down the hall to his bedroom, his fingers woven through hers in a firm grip.

Once there, he touched a wall switch, bathing the king-sized bed in a warm glow from lamps on the nightstands. His gaze was steady and his movements sure as he undressed her. Only the slight tremble of his fingers and the ragged sound of his breathing hinted at the emotions he was keeping tightly leashed.

She stood still, moving only when he needed her to, but inside she was anything but still. Blood rushed through her veins, whipped to a frenzy by the frantic thump of her heart. Her breasts ached and her core throbbed. Every breath took effort, and the lack of oxygen made her dizzy. She was melting, immersed in the liquid of desire.

When he'd taken away everything, including the scrunchie holding her ponytail in place, he lifted her gently in his arms and laid her on the puckered surface of a soft quilt. Then he started on his clothes.

His movements grew less and less precise. Clearly impatient with the buttons on his shirt, he yanked hard and a button flew.

Turning her head in his direction, she sucked in breath after breath as he shed his jeans and briefs. What moron would deprive herself of *that*? Talk about cruel and unusual punishment.

As he approached the bed, he reached for the handle on the nightstand drawer. He paused. His low, sexy chuckle created swirls of excitement in her stomach.

Heat simmered in his dark eyes. "Can you believe I forgot?"

"Want to wear one for old time's sake?"

"Take a guess." He climbed in and moved over her. Dipping his head, he gave her a slow, sensual kiss. He ended it gradually, nibbling on her lips. "Let's keep it simple. We'll get creative later."

His husky murmur made her shiver. "We will?" Sliding her hands up his back, she clutched his broad shoulders, her quivering body ready, so ready.

"That's a promise. But right now, I don't need fancy."

"Me, either."

"Just this." Braced on his forearms, his gaze locked with hers, he pushed deep.

And her world made sense again. This connection felt so real, so good, even more wonderful than she remembered. How could that be when they'd had the ultimate experience of creating a child?

His breath hitched and he closed his eyes, his lashes dark against his cheek. When he opened them and looked down at her, emotion flickered there. "It's even better."

"I know."

"I didn't expect that." He slowly began to stroke. "I didn't... ahh, Brittany... I love how you move with me."

"Because I want..."

"You want me. You want this." His eyes glowed with happiness. "Even though we've already—"

"*Yes*." Focusing on him, giving her answer with her body, she lifted her hips to meet his thrusts as the rhythmic friction worked its magic, taking her higher, and higher yet.

This beautiful man had given her a child and now he was giving her pleasure. So much pleasure. Her core tightened as he moved faster, bearing down.

"Let go, Brittany," he crooned softly.

And she did, digging her fingers into his back and crying out as the waves of her climax crashed over her.

He followed, her name on his lips as he shuddered, his pulsing tempo matching hers.

Glorious.

Breathing hard, he leaned his forehead against hers. "I want you to spend the night."

"Okay."

He lifted his head and sucked in air. "That was easy."

"I like it here."

"In my bed or in my cabin?"

"Both."

"Excellent. Then how about coming out Friday night and staying with me until Sunday morning?"

A faint warning light flashed. "Why?"

He started laughing, which created a very interesting sensation as his laughter shook... everything. "I think that's obvious."

So he wanted more of this. Understandable. "We can't stay in bed all day and night."

He grinned. "We can't? Shoot. Guess we'll have to find a wedding to go to."

"Oh, that's right. Saturday's the wedding."

"You forgot? Damn, I'm good."

She got a kick out of this playful side of him. "You did make me forget, but don't let it go to your head."

"Too late. You're in for it, now."

Lowering her voice to a soft purr, she batted her eyelashes. "Oh, I hope so."

His breath caught. "Keep that up and I might just stay where I am and start over."

"Fine with me."

He held her gaze, heat building in his dark eyes. "No getting around it, I'm obsessed with you."

"Backatcha."

"I'd ask for the whole weekend, but Sunday is Mother's Day."

"Right. I always spend it with my mom."

"And I'll be with mine. Although it would be entirely appropriate to be with you, too. I just don't think that's feasible."

"Probably not."

Leaning down, he kissed the corners of her mouth, then the top lip and the bottom. "So will you?" He repeated the routine. "I told Desiree I might bring someone to the wedding rehearsal Friday night. Now she'll be expecting me to bring you."

"I like it when you kiss me like that."

"Then I'll keep doing it." He sucked lightly on her lower lip.

"But I can't think."

He raised his head again. "Then I'll stop."

She also had trouble thinking when they were still snugly joined, but she didn't want him to move. She liked that feeling. A lot. Maybe they could just start over without changing positions.

His patience was nice, too. He didn't bug her for an answer, just let her take her time deciding.

Really, it was a no-brainer. "Well, since the wedding's out here and I'm going to it, I suppose staying with you Friday and Saturday night makes sense."

"Wow, don't you sound excited."

"It's just that we'll be going public. I mean really public, and I thought we weren't going to do that until after the wedding."

"I know that was the original plan, but it looks like we're already coloring outside the lines." He shifted his hips, emphasizing the point.

"Maybe not as much as you think."

"We're in bed together. That wasn't supposed to happen."

"No, but in a way, I'm following Desiree's advice."

His eyes lit with amusement. "By ending the cruel and unusual punishment?"

"Partly. I asked how we were supposed to get to the platonic friendship stage if we were hopping into bed all the time."

"I can't wait to hear how she answered that."

"She said we had to work it out and find a solution that was mutually satisfying."

"No magic formula, then. Big surprise."

"But she also said this. You'll never have a reasonable discussion with a sexually frustrated man. And I realized—"

"That's why we're here?" He stared at her, all traces of humor gone. "So you can have a reasonable discussion with me?"

"It doesn't only apply to you. I've been frustrated, too. I wasn't any more capable of a reasonable discussion than you were."

"Then all we're doing here is letting off steam so we can figure out how to have a non-sexual relationship?"

"It's not just about that. I can't speak for you, but this connection we have is special and although I don't see it as a long-term—"

"If it's so special, why are you so damned eager to get rid of it?"

"I'm not *eager*. But the whole idea was to avoid any kind of romantic entanglement, and if we're—"

"You know what? I didn't take a good look at the fire before we left the living room. I need to go check on it." He was out of bed in no time. Grabbing his jeans and briefs off the floor, he ducked into the bathroom.

She sat up, anxiety burning in her chest. "Hey, Trent, I'm sorry. I probably shouldn't have told you what she said. I thought you might think it was funny, but my timing was awful."

No answer. Moments later he came out of the bathroom wearing his jeans. "I might have thought it was funny if I didn't also get the distinct impression you viewed this last encounter as a means to an end."

"I swear I wasn't thinking of it that way! I wanted to make love to you!"

"But then you did think of it that way or you wouldn't have said you were following her advice. And guess what? We're sexually satisfied and now we're fighting." He left the room.

Great. This was exactly the kind of drama she was trying to avoid. She put a hand on her stomach. He was upset, and looking at it from his standpoint, he had reason.

She had to fix this. They were going to have a baby in nine months, and they were going to be friends when that happened. She'd make sure of it.

27

Instead of making sure the fire was out, Trent got it going again. Maybe he'd end up spending the night on the sofa. Wouldn't that be a kick in the head?

The logs caught fast, almost as fast as their cozy situation had turned to ashes. He flopped down on the sofa. The remains of their half-finished dinner stared him in the face, taunting him with the moment when he'd decided to take Brittany to bed.

You'll never have a reasonable discussion with a sexually frustrated man.

He had to believe she hadn't been thinking that when she'd given him the look that had led to another incredible round of... he didn't know what to call it, but he wanted that experience more than he wanted to breathe.

And not with just anyone. The soul-stirring emotion that swept over him when he buried himself deep was all tied in with Brittany — the way she moved, the scent of her body, the light in her blue eyes, the silky texture of her hair fanned out on the pillow.

Did it mean as much to her as it did to him? It couldn't or she wouldn't be clinging to this platonic friendship deal they'd made.

His chest heaved. He'd agreed to it. At the time, considering the horror his marriage had turned into, he'd bought the idea of a friends-only relationship while they raised their kid. He wanted that kid, no matter what it took.

Looked like it would take giving up what he'd just experienced a few minutes ago. To be fair, that hadn't been part of the original deal. Only a bonus, something that was necessary to the process and would provide temporary fun.

Fun. Carnival rides were fun. Joking around with his brother was fun. Cantering across the meadow on Gigabyte was fun.

What he shared with Brittany fit into a whole different category. Maybe he should think of it as a luxury, a pleasure he'd been lucky enough to enjoy because of special circumstances but not something that would ever be a permanent part of his life.

The whisper of bare feet on the wood floor made him look up. Brittany stood behind the easy chair wearing his shirt and clutching the teddy bear he'd bought for Montana.

The lady knew how to deliver a sucker punch. He stood. "I'm sorry. I shouldn't have flown off the handle like that."

"No, *I'm* sorry. It was a stupid thing to say. It made it sound like I was manipulating you with sex. I would never do that. I hate the idea of leading a man around by his—"

"Except you could." He swallowed. "I think that's what scares the hell out of me. Cheryl manipulated me with sex at first, but once I figured out her hidden agenda, it didn't work anymore. You, on the other hand...."

"It's because of the baby."

"That's part of it, but there's more going on. Just now had nothing to do with the baby. I didn't think about her once."

"I didn't either. I swear I didn't. Or our agreement. Or what Desiree said. It was only later, when we started talking."

"I believe you. If you were devious, Rance would have warned me."

"Rance? Have you told him?"

"No. Before he left the Buffalo Saturday night, he suggested I should get to know you. He pointed out that you were giving me the eye."

"Which I was. When you took a break and walked back to the bathroom, I mentally undressed you."

"Oh?" He certainly didn't mind hearing that. "Coming or going?"

"Both."

"I doubt you were thinking platonic friendship when you were ogling me."

"Nope." Her smile bloomed. "I was thinking *hot stuff.*"

He gazed at her, his heart swelling. Other parts of him swelled, too. "I think it's possible your plan was doomed from the start."

"It's very possible."

"Want to come over and sit down? I think we need to have a reasonable discussion."

"Can I bring Sage?"

"Sage?"

"I looked at this bear with her red bandana and thought *Sage,* but since you bought her...."

"Sage is good. By all means bring her. We could use some wisdom."

"And her name sounds Western, to go with the bandana." She walked around the chair. "But if you already named her, just tell me."

"I didn't. I'm glad you came up with one. Every teddy bear needs a name." His shirttail reached almost to her knees, so technically everything was covered. That didn't stop him from visualizing what was under that shirt.

"I hope you don't mind that I went looking for her."

"I don't, but why did you?"

"I thought she'd help keep us focused."

"Then you probably should have put on more than my shirt."

"I understand what you're saying, but there's a reason I wore it. There's a button missing, by the way."

"I know."

Walking past the hearth, she rounded the coffee table and sat in the same spot she'd taken for their previous discussion before dinner. She put the bear on her lap.

Since it was about fourteen inches tall, he didn't need much imagination to picture her holding a baby that size. "Why'd you wear the shirt?"

She glanced up at him. "Are you going to sit down?"

"Yes. I just haven't decided where."

"You can sit beside me."

"Thanks for the invitation, but I'm gonna take the easy chair." He settled into it and kept his attention on her face and the bear. Straying lower would give him a view of her knees and a tempting glimpse of creamy thighs. That wouldn't be helpful.

The back cushion of the leather chair felt weird when he wasn't wearing a shirt, so he leaned forward a little. "Okay, why the shirt?"

"I couldn't find a bathrobe in your closet."

"I don't own one."

"So I found out. That's why I'm wearing this. It's the most efficient thing since I expect we'll be getting naked again soon."

He sucked in a breath. "Why?"

"To steal your line, I think that's obvious."

"Not to me. The way I look at this, we might as well bite the bullet."

"We've proven that doesn't work. It's too soon. We like making love too much."

"But if we'll eventually have to give it up, I'd rather—"

"Are you sure?"

His brother's words echoed in his head. *Just go with it.* "No, but to continue a sexual relationship with the end looming ever closer doesn't sound great, either."

"It's like dealing with any habit."

"No, it's not. That I can say for sure."

"Just hear me out. I agree that my old plan was doomed. You turn me on and vice versa. I didn't take that into consideration and I should have. My excitement about the baby blinded me to the obvious fly in the ointment."

"That makes two of us. I'll share responsibility for that lack of foresight."

"I'm glad we didn't have foresight, because now we'll have a baby. If we'd figured out we were asking for trouble, we wouldn't have jumped off that cliff in the first place."

And he would have likely gone through life never knowing the joy of what they'd experienced together. "That's a valid point, but now the bun's in the oven and we've pinpointed our mistake. Shouldn't we just quit now and be done with it?"

"I don't want to."

"Neither do I! But—"

"Here's my new plan. We enjoy each other tonight. Then I come back Friday night and stay until Sunday morning, like you said. We spend as much time in bed as we can, considering we'll be attending all the festivities."

"And will we also have a whole lot of reasonable discussions?"

"I'd rather not have any discussions, at least not any heavy ones."

He'd have a tough time rejecting what sounded like heaven on earth. "Then what?"

"Then we set up a schedule that coincides with when you're working at the Buffalo so that we can get together at my house a couple of times during the week. Then we'll probably end up out here on weekends."

"Something you should know. If I told Clint I wanted to work every weeknight, he'd let me."

"That would be counterproductive. The goal is to create spaces in our time together and gradually increase the size of those spaces."

"And you think that will work?"

"It's how I weaned myself off diet soda."

He had the urge to laugh, but her expression was so endearingly earnest that he controlled himself. He didn't think she was right about this, though.

Their intense lovemaking was nothing like slugging down a can of diet soda. It was more like drinking from a firehose.

Which reminded him of Dallas and his advice to just go with it. What choice did he have? If he rejected her carefully constructed plan, they'd both be miserable, which would cause his folks and Dallas to worry during what was supposed to be a time of celebration.

Might as well follow his big brother's advice.

_28_

Would her plan work? Brit had no idea, but for the time being, Trent was a happy man. Until the fire died down, they were restricted to the living room. That made the sofa their best option, so he fetched a blanket so they wouldn't slide around on the leather upholstery.

Making love had never been so funny. Afterward they ate the rest of their dinner and cleaned up the dishes.

By then the fire was almost out and they returned to his king-sized bed, their hunger for each other still strong. At last they slept, sated and content wrapped in each other's arms.

She slipped out of bed at dawn, careful not to disturb him, and took her clothes into the bathroom. As she was washing up, the scent of coffee brewing drifted under the closed door.

He'd stocked up on non-alcoholic beer. Had he picked up decaf coffee, too? Dressing quickly, she hurried into the kitchen, where he was in the process of pouring a cup from the carafe.

Glancing up, he smiled and held it out. "Decaf."

"Thank you! But why did you buy it? You didn't know I'd be here in the morning."

"Sure didn't." He gestured toward a bag of coffee from the counter. "That's for you to take home. You didn't have any yesterday and since you were coming here right after work, you wouldn't have had time to shop."

"What a lovely thing to do." Waking up to coffee and the sight of Trent in jeans and an unbuttoned shirt took the sting out of leaving his cozy bed. His unshaven jaw conjured up good memories, too. "Desiree's right. You'll make a fantastic dad."

"Thanks for giving me the option." He started to say something, then closed his mouth again.

"What?"

He sighed. "I'm probably a damned fool for bringing this up, but something Dallas said as he was going out the door last night keeps running through my mind."

"About having a second one?"

"You heard that, too?"

"I did."

"I'm one of four and you're an only. I liked having siblings, mostly, except when one of them would get on my very last nerve. Were you okay with being an only?"

"Nope. I tortured my poor mother begging for a brother or sister. I didn't care which. I didn't know she kept trying after I was born but no dice."

"So how do you feel about Montana being an only?"

"Not good, but she's a start."

He grinned. "I was afraid it was a dangerous topic."

"Not really. Desiree set a precedent there, too. Bret and Gil have the same father."

"Actually I did know that. But not the story behind it."

"Faye talked about it during one of our birthday dinners at the Buffalo. The boys figure their dad was a fun bed partner but he and Desiree had nothing in common. They had the good sense to admit it and he didn't stick around, but when she wanted another baby, she contacted him and he was willing."

"Well, you have my number."

She smiled. "And you've got mine. In all respects. I've had a wonderful time."

"Me, too. I miss you already and you haven't walked out the door."

"But I need to." She drained her coffee and set the cup on the counter. "That was delicious. Tasted just like regular."

"The guy at the market said this was the best decaf brand he had." He picked it up and handed it to her. Then he wrapped an arm around her shoulders. "I'll walk you to the door."

"That would be nice."

"What time can you get here Friday?"

"My last appointment's at three. If I pack a few things in advance, I should be able to be out here no later than four."

"Good. That gives us a little time before we go over for the rehearsal at five."

She glanced up at him. "I'll arrive dressed for the evening, so—"

"I know. I'm not planning to seduce you. We'll just talk. I can tell you how my folks took the news before you'll be coming face-to-face with them."

"And I can tell you how my mom takes the news when I tell her I'm spending Friday and Saturday night with you."

"You know what? I could drive in and pick you up on Friday afternoon. Then I can take you back home early Sunday morning. That's a classier way to do it."

"That's the gas-guzzling way to do it."

"But I want to. Sending you off like this feels wrong."

She turned to face him. "Because you have a knight in shining armor complex."

"Not really. I just—"

"No, really. And I'm grateful, because if you hadn't insisted on driving me home Saturday night, we wouldn't be standing here right now."

"I guess you're right."

"So sure, come and pick me up on Friday. I'll leave the key under the mat so if you get there before I do, just let yourself in. I'll see you then." Sliding her hand behind his neck, she rose on tiptoe and kissed him.

With a soft groan, he kissed her back, gathering her close. Then he released her slowly and opened the door. "Drive carefully."

"You, too." She shivered as a cool breeze touched skin flushed from his kiss.

"Want a jacket? A blanket?"

"No, thanks. I'll just run to the truck." Resisting the impulse to kiss him again, she dashed across the porch and down the steps.

Her truck cab was cold after sitting there all night. Closing the door quickly, she set the coffee on the passenger seat and started the engine. She also turned on the heater, although it wouldn't do anything yet.

She would bring a warm jacket out here for the weekend. Summer wasn't here yet. She put the truck in reverse and checked her rearview mirror as she backed out so she could turn around.

When she started the turn, she glanced over at the cabin. Trent stood on the porch, barefoot, his shirt still unbuttoned and his hands shoved in the front pockets of his jeans. He lifted one hand and flashed the smile that had dazzled her Saturday night. She had a thing for good teeth.

She tapped the horn and drove away, watching in the rearview mirror until the trees blocked her view. She had a thing for Trent Armstrong, too. And it went way beyond friendship.

<u>29</u>

Dallas was waiting on the porch when Trent drove up at ten on the dot. They'd been raised to be punctual and those lessons had stuck.

The minute he was in and buckled up, Trent pulled away and glanced over at his brother. "Well?"

He dragged in a breath. "You were right. You were so right. Thank God we talked about it last night. It was *awesome.* I had no idea. *She* had no idea. She says we couldn't have made a baby, though, because the timing's off, but damn, we had fun."

Trent chuckled. "Told you."

"To think I advised you against this move of yours. If you'd listened to me, you wouldn't have had that experience, and you wouldn't have told me about it. Angie and I would have put this off. Maybe even a year or two. I hate to even think about missing out for another two years."

"Then you and Cheyenne will be adjusting your work schedules?"

"I'll talk to him about it first chance I get. Our schedules are jacked up anyway, so it might as well be now. We rearranged our shifts for the wedding so we're on call today and tomorrow, but off on Saturday. The chief's been great about working around this event."

"Like Brittany said, it's Wagon Train's wedding of the century."

"You should probably call her Brit, dude. At least in public."

"Why?"

"Because the way you say her name, it sounds like you're madly in love with her even though you claim that's not the case."

"You're reading too much into it."

"Speaking of that, what happened after we left? Did she toddle on home after dinner?"

"Nope."

Dallas grinned. "No more cruel and unusual punishment?"

"Angie must have filled you in on the rest of Desiree's advice."

"Uh-huh. But she waited until the walk home to tell me that part. She knew I'd laugh and she didn't think we should be yukking it up in your kitchen, all things considered."

"And did you laugh?"

"Oh, yeah. So loud I scattered a flock of quail roosting in a tree." He switched to falsetto. "*You can't have a reasonable discussion with a sexually deprived man.* Classic Desiree."

"Sexually *frustrated* man."

"Whatever. Deprived. Frustrated. Same thing. She's so right."

"Yeah, and I got into an argument with Brittany over it."

"You had a fight? From what you said, I thought—"

"My fault. I started it."

"Because you were sexually frustrated?"

"No, I— never mind. We made up. We had fun last night, too."

"I'm glad to hear it. Let the good times roll."

"Unfortunately, that's not how she sees it. She's worked out a timetable to wean us off that activity."

"What the hell?"

"She wants us to be platonic buddies by the time Montana's born."

"I don't see that happening. I get it now, and I can't imagine—"

"It's not a terrible idea."

"Yes, it is, bro. Worst idea ever."

"Think about this. If I'd made the mistake of having a kid with Cheryl—"

"Condoms were invented for women like Cheryl. Thank God you used them and none of them broke."

"But what if one had? That baby's life would have been hell. We would have ended up divorced, anyway, and the fighting would never have stopped because we'd have this kid to argue about."

"But Brit is not Cheryl, in case you hadn't noticed."

"And I'm not like her dad, who left her mom and married someone else when she was around ten. That really affected her."

"I didn't know about that. Unfortunate."

"She's worried that continuing to get horizontal might lead to romance."

"She's not wrong. We're taught love is supposed to come before sex, but sometimes it's the other way around."

"Which is why I'll go along with her plan, because I'm not looking for romance any more than she is."

Dallas glanced at him, then turned away to gaze out the side window. But he hadn't moved fast enough to hide his smile.

"I'm not, damn it."

"Okay." He focused on the rural landscape for several minutes. "How's the grand opening shaping up for L'Amour and More in Apple Grove?"

"Good." He was happy to change the subject. "There's only one marketing angle I can't make happen. I think it would be huge but it looks like we'll have to do without it."

"What's that?"

"M.R. Morrison's an *NYT* bestseller and the folks in Apple Grove love his books, not to mention tourists who'll be in town by then. An in-person signing event would put that shop on the map, but damned if I can break through the wall of mystery surrounding the guy."

"That's too bad."

"He lives somewhere in Montana. I can't prove it, but since moving here I've read enough of his books to be convinced he's from this area. The way he writes about the Sapphires you'd swear he was staring right at that mountain range while he's typing."

"Yes, you would."

"I stopped by Desiree and Andy's table yesterday when I was in the Buffalo and mentioned how much I'd like to find the guy. Andy said they were making progress, like he knew something I didn't. Which reminds me. What was going on last night when Angie bragged about Desiree's ability to keep secrets?"

"What do you mean?"

"When Angie said her mom was a world champion secret-keeper, you said *that's for damn sure*, like you'd personally experienced it. And Angie tensed. Is something going on I don't know about?"

When Dallas didn't answer, Trent glanced at him.

His brother was staring straight ahead, unmoving except for when his jaw muscle flexed.

"I take it there is."

"I can't talk about it."

"Is there a gold mine somewhere on the property? That would explain why she's so well-off." He was only half-joking. He'd picked up bits and pieces of info since January and nothing added up unless she was an investment genius. But why would she keep quiet about that, especially around her family?

"I really can't say anything, bro. I would if I could, but—"

"Okay. I'll leave it alone." But he'd keep his eyes and ears open. After Andy had said *I think we're making progress,* he'd looked over at Desiree. Was M.R. Morrison one of her ex-boyfriends?

"Thanks, dude. Appreciate it." Dallas cleared his throat. "Why were you in the Buffalo?"

"Meeting Brittany's mom."

"I didn't hear about that. How'd it go?"

Describing the lunch conversation brought them to the subject of what exactly he'd say to their parents on the way back. They were still discussing it as they neared the airport and Dallas got a text from their mom that the plane had landed a few minutes early.

Trent scored a parking space near the bag claim entrance, and they made it inside just as their dad hauled a big suitcase off the conveyor belt. While Dallas hurried over to grab it for him, Trent hugged his mom.

She was tall, nearly five-ten. When he was small she used to crouch down to hug him. Now he hunched over a little to hug her.

The scent of her favorite perfume brought a lump to his throat. She was the only person in the world who'd seen him cry when he talked about leaving Cheryl. The tears hadn't been for Cheryl. He'd cried because she'd killed his favorite dream.

30

Brit clued her mother in that they needed another break-time discussion to bring her up to date. She hadn't mentioned the trip to Rowdy Ranch to her mom the day before because she hadn't decided whether she'd follow through.

At least that's what she'd told herself. Maybe she'd suspected all along that she wouldn't be able to stay away. And wouldn't want to leave.

The possibility of spending the night had hovered in the back of her mind from the moment he'd invited her to his cabin. He'd likely had the same thought, despite his attempt to neutralize the visit by inviting Angie and Dallas.

That they craved each other way more than they'd expected was a problem. If she glossed over it, she wouldn't be doing either of them any favors. She'd start by being completely honest with her mom about this attraction and why she wanted to nip it in the bud.

She brought a thermos of decaf into the break room after wrapping up her nine-o'clock appointment. Her mom wasn't there yet.

She popped in a few minutes later. "Sorry. I had someone who had to reschedule and it took a while to get them squared away. Let me get my coffee." She glanced at Brit's thermos. "Decaf?"

"Yes, ma'am." She grabbed a cup, sat down and opened the thermos. The aroma of the coffee Trent had bought her was subtly different from Doc Bradbury's choice for the break room.

Breathing it in sent a shiver of longing through her. Tasting it brought back the memory of their goodbye kiss at the door. She missed him.

Her mother took a seat on the other side of the small table and cradled her cup in both hands. "Fire away."

She put down her cup. "As usual, you called it. I spent the night out at Rowdy Ranch."

"Color me shocked." Her mom took a sip of her coffee. "I figured that would happen. Either that or he'd come to your house. So what now?"

"He asked me to come out Friday night for the rehearsal dinner and stay until early Sunday morning. That means I won't be driving out there with you and the doc on Saturday."

She nodded. "None of this surprises me. Not after seeing you two together yesterday."

"Also, I can't remember if I told you his parents are flying out for the wedding."

"Oh, they are? No, you didn't mention it."

"Do you want to meet them? It'll be a huge crowd, so if you'd rather not...."

"Let me think about it. Is he telling them about the baby?"

"Yes. He and Dallas are picking them up this morning. He'll tell them on the way back."

"Then I should meet them. If he was planning to keep it a secret, I might have avoided it in case I let something slip. I guess you'll meet them at the rehearsal, then."

"For the second time. I had a brief conversation with them at Angie's wedding, but I doubt they remember me."

"What are they like?"

"Tall. Nice looking. Vanessa's hair was light brown in February, but I'm sure she colors it so it might be different now. Harry's is salt and pepper like yours. They seem like good people."

"They probably are if Trent plans to tell them. It sounds like he trusts them not to overreact and disrupt the festive weekend."

"I hadn't thought of it that way, but you're right."

"If you stayed through Sunday you could get to know them better."

"No way. I'll be back for our Mother's Day celebration. It's important to me."

"Me, too, but—"

"I'll be here. We'll cook and watch movies like we always do. If you have time, maybe you can dig out those softball pictures so we can look through them."

She smiled, the crease of worry between her eyebrows fading. "I'll do that."

"Speaking of trusting people to keep their cool, I talked with Desiree while I was out there."

Her eyebrows rose and she put down her coffee. "How did that happen? Isn't she knee-deep in wedding frenzy?"

"Not so much. Dallas and Angie had dinner with us, and they both urged me to go see her and get her advice. Angie rode over with me and the discussion was...intense."

"I'll bet. So what did she say?"

"Kind of what you said, that the original plan Trent and I agreed to isn't realistic. So I've come up with a new one — to continue our physical relationship for now but gradually taper off."

"Gradually taper off." It was a comment, not a question.

"You're not buying it."

"No, can't say that I am. But honey, if you can manage it, more power to you. He's down on marriage and you aren't excited about it, either, so maybe you two can successfully deescalate the situation."

"I believe we can. I'm not saying it will be easy. But it's for the best."

"I just wish..." Her mom trailed off and then she sighed. "Maybe this is my issue, not yours."

"What?"

"I've always wished you'd fall deeply in love with someone worthy of you, someone you couldn't wait to see every day who would give you joy and make you want to build a life together. I didn't find my soul mate, but I've hoped maybe you would."

"I haven't yet."

"Are you sure? Because when you're with Trent, it's like there's a magnetic force at work."

"It's static cling. The shirt I wore yesterday was polyester."

"Very funny. I guess all I was sensing was sexual chemistry. He can't be the right one since he doesn't believe in happily ever after."

"Neither do I." She said it softly, but her mother still flinched. "It's not your fault. Or Dad's. It's me. I have ridiculously high standards. I might eventually find someone who measures up, but in the meantime, I won't miss out on parenthood."

"Would you be willing to tell me what your ridiculously high standards are? I don't think I've ever heard them."

"Okay. Sure. He's kind. I mean to the max. To people, animals, all living things. He's intelligent but not a know-it-all and not threatened by smart women. He'll scrub a toilet, change a diaper and wash windows. He can laugh at himself, is considerate in bed and looks good naked." She paused to take a breath.

"That's it?"

"Mostly, except he has to love Wagon Train 'cause I'm not leaving, and it would be a bonus if we had a couple of activities in common. Oh, and if he's curious about things, that would be nice. It's logical he'd be fun to talk with."

"That's a great list. So if you found someone like that, you'd marry him?"

"Assuming I'm also wildly attracted to him and we have a great time between the sheets. Trent's set the gold standard, there."

"Does he fulfill any of your other requirements?"

"I can't say. There's a lot I don't know about him. But even if he ticks all the boxes, you just said it. He's had a wife and never wants another one. He thinks romance is for suckers."

"So you'll be driving out there after work tomorrow?"

"Actually, no. He wants to pick me up."

"Because he'll be in town running errands?"

"I don't think so. He didn't mention that."

"Then won't he have to bring you in on Sunday and then drive all the way back out to Rowdy Ranch?"

"Yes, and it makes no sense. I told him he'd use twice the gas I would use. More than twice because I doubt his rig gets the mileage mine does. But if it makes him happy, who am I to argue?"

"Hmm."

"I guess he just likes driving that truck."

"I'm sure that's it." Her lips twitched, as if she was holding back a smile.

"All right, I'll admit he has a tendency to play the knight in shining armor role."

"Because there's certainly nothing romantic about that."

"It's one of those silly contradictions. Everyone has 'em. It doesn't mean he'll suddenly drop to one knee and propose."

"Of course not." Her mom finished her coffee and stood.

Brit did the same and pretended not to notice the twinkle in her mom's eyes. She'd just decided Trent wasn't a lost cause, after all.

But that wasn't what made Brit's stomach churn or her hand shake as she twisted the top back on her thermos. She'd just created a mental image of Trent on one knee asking her for her hand in marriage.

That would ruin everything.

31

Trent's parents totally believed his statement that Brittany was pregnant. They loved the name Montana, which they said would work regardless of whether the baby turned out to be a girl or a boy.

That was the good news. The bad news? They were totally against the two-household, platonic friendship plan for raising that baby. They made their objections clear all the way back to Wagon Train.

But once they stepped through the door of Desiree's house, all discussion on the topic ended. Desiree didn't bring it up, either. Trent assumed Andy had the info by now, but he certainly wouldn't be the one to say something.

Angie joined them for lunch and she didn't say a word about it, either. After they ate, all seven of them went riding, which allowed him to introduce his folks to Gigabyte. That went well. If only their meeting with Brittany would go as smoothly. He wasn't optimistic.

Then came the potluck dinner he'd forgotten about. The whole family showed up, and he spent the evening watching his every word.

That sucked, especially with Rance. He'd been a good friend and deserved to know what was going on.

The party started breaking up after dessert. His folks were tired and everyone was intent on resting up in preparation for a busy weekend. Before his mom and dad headed down the hallway toward their room, Trent hugged them each goodnight.

"It'll all work out, son." His dad squeezed his shoulder. "Don't worry."

"What he said." His mom smiled. "I can't wait to meet her."

"I think you did in February."

"Then I'm sure I'll recognize her when she comes for the rehearsal. Tell her we're looking forward to seeing her again."

"I will." He had plenty more to tell her. And a request.

He offered to help with cleanup, but the gang had everything under control so he headed out. He took the ranch road slow to avoid the night critters, his muscles tight with impatience.

Finally he was inside his cabin and could pull out his phone. He hadn't said he'd call her and he had no idea if she'd be home or not. She could be over at her mom's. He hoped not.

She answered on the first ring. "Hi, Trent."

"Where are you?"

"Standing in front of my closet trying to decide what to wear to the wedding."

He sucked in a breath. She would have to mention a closet.

"Where are you?"

"In my living room wishing I could be there so we could make use of your closet."

"You need to ditch that fantasy. I doubt it's nearly as much fun as you're imagining. You might throw your back out."

"Have you ever done it in a closet?"

"No, but—"

"Then how do you know?"

"I've never done it outside during a blizzard, either, and I know for a fact it would put my body in danger."

"But what a way to go. I know which part of me would freeze last."

"Is this your version of a dirty phone call?"

"Maybe. Is it working?"

"I'm not going to tell you."

"That means it is. I can be there in thirty minutes."

"Don't come."

"I'll hang on until I get there."

She laughed. "Stop it. Don't tease."

"I'm not teasing. I doubt any cops are patrolling that road on a Thursday night. I could make it in twenty." He could already taste her kisses and feel the warmth of her—

"Stay where you are, please."

"Really?"

"Yes, really."

"Hang on a sec. I need to apologize to my buddy. He's easily excited."

"Don't I know it."

He took a deep breath and cleared his throat. "Alrighty, let's start over. I had a reason to call. I need your permission to tell Rance. He should be home by now. I'd like to go over and talk to him tonight."

"Then you weren't serious about driving into town to see me?"

"Oh, I was dead serious. If you'd said yes, I would have figured out a time to catch him tomorrow. I have my priorities. Want to reconsider?"

On the other end, her breath hitched. "No. We need sleep."

"You're probably right. I just miss you."

"Same here."

The tender way she said it made him long to wrap her in his arms. What if he promised to just hold her while they fell asleep? Could he do that? Yeah, probably not.

"Why do you want to tell Rance tonight?"

"He's the one I'm closest to out here, except for Dallas. We just finished up a family gathering and it bothered me that he doesn't know. I don't want him getting the news when the rest of them do. He deserves to hear it from me ahead of time."

"Then by all means tell him. Just ask him to keep it to himself."

"I will."

"Just so you know, he has a reputation as the family rabble-rouser."

"And I've seen that side of him. I also trust him. There's a lot going on under the surface with that guy. He's more solid than most people think."

"I'll respect your judgment on it, then. You know, if you're telling Rance, I should probably talk to Ella."

"I get that, but you might not want to contact her tonight. She was yawning at dinner and said she was going straight to bed when she gets home."

"And her PE classes start early in the morning. Maybe I can find a time at the rehearsal. Hey, you haven't mentioned your parents, yet. Did they get here okay?"

"Sure did. My mom said to tell you she's looking forward to seeing you again."

"She remembers me?"

"Not specifically, but she knows she'll recognize you once she sees you again."

She responded with a chuckle.

He smiled. "Come on. She will. She—"

"Your mom doesn't remember me, but that's okay. She had enough on her plate keeping track of all the McLintocks. Never mind about that. What was their reaction to the pregnancy announcement?"

"At first they were stunned. Not that they didn't believe it, but... not my usual behavior."

"I'm sure."

"But they warmed up to it fast. Naturally they're hoping this supposed friendship agreement will morph into something else."

"Just like my mom."

"Yep. I don't know if we'll get any of them to understand that angle, although it helps that Desiree had the same idea. They're also really excited about the baby and they love the name Montana."

"So their reaction was mostly positive."

"It was. But like I said, they don't like that we'll maintain separate households. They never said the M word, but they think a child does better when the parents live together."

"Even after meeting the McLintock gang?"

"They said Buck and Marybeth made a huge difference and having a bunch of kids helped, too. When I mentioned divorced parents, they said divorced parents aren't often good friends. If we like each other, living together shouldn't be a problem."

"It's a logical argument except for one thing."

"I wasn't going to say we can't keep our hands off each other. Not when I'm doing seventy with my beloved family members in the truck."

"Good grief! I wouldn't want you telling them that while we're sitting around enjoying a warm beverage."

"I won't have to tell them since Desiree's fully informed. I guarantee we'll be the main topic of conversation at breakfast tomorrow morning. And I'll come up with a good excuse not to be there."

"Maybe hearing it from Desiree is for the best." She let out a sigh. "I really didn't think this through. I pictured it as a private matter between the two of us. It's anything but."

"Listen, if you're worried about me telling Rance, I'll—"

"No, go ahead."

"Then I'd better hang up before it gets any later. See you tomorrow afternoon."

"See you then."

"Feels like forever."

"I know. G'night."

"Sweet dreams." He forced himself to tap the disconnect button. Then he texted Rance.

He texted right back and said he'd open a couple of beers. With a silent apology to Brittany, he sent back a thumbs-up emoji.

Rance's log cabin had some features similar to the others — a rock fireplace on the wall opposite the front door, a kitchen to the left and two bedrooms down the hall, a primary and a guest room. But instead of a sofa and chairs in his living/dining area, Rance had a pool table.

He'd only had it a couple of months, and to make space, he'd moved the sofa into his guest room and placed the easy chairs against one wall. Four dining chairs were lined up along the opposite one. No telling what he'd done with the dining table.

The only other furniture in the room was an antique rolltop desk and matching chair. The desk was a little too tall and blocked the lower third of a large window that looked out on the porch. But it wasn't so high that it ruined a premium view of the Sapphires.

Rance handed him a beer the minute he walked through the door. "Glad you came. I could tell something was on your mind tonight. Something you didn't want to bring up with everyone around."

"There is." He took one swig and then started talking. He paced back and forth, gesturing with the bottle, until he'd given Rance the whole complicated picture, including the work glove reference to explain how he knew Brittany was pregnant.

At last he was done. Pausing, he looked at Rance. "So, what do you think? Does her plan stand a snowball's chance in hell of succeeding?"

Rance grinned. "You know the answer."

"I suppose I do." He took another sip of the beer. "Any advice?"

"Do the program."

"Should I tell her I don't think it'll work?"

"This isn't about telling, dude. It's about showing."

32

Brit had been jumpy ever since she'd climbed out of bed this morning, and the butterflies were having a field day in her stomach by the time she pulled into the driveway of her rented bungalow around four-fifteen. Trent's blue F-250 sat at the curb, gleaming in the sunlight. No doubt he'd washed it.

The man himself had chosen to wait for her on the porch steps. She'd had chairs out there last summer but she retired those weather-beaten relics and hadn't bought new ones.

He unfolded his six-foot-three frame and stood as she braked her truck in front of the garage that had once housed Model-Ts and was too small for even her vehicle.

He had a bit of a cowboy swagger as he strolled across the grass toward her, his prize-winning smile sending those butterflies whirling even faster. His hat shaded his eyes, but not enough to disguise the heat smoldering there.

He opened her door. "Thought you'd never get here."

"Blame Mr. Abernathy. He never flosses." She sounded like a breathless teenager. Her fingers wouldn't work right as she struggled with the release for the seatbelt. What was it with him and seatbelts?

"Allow me." Ducking down so he wouldn't knock off his hat, he reached across her lap, bringing the earthy aroma of his aftershave closer as he neatly unsnapped the buckle.

Her heart rate tripled. "Don't kiss me."

"Not gonna." He didn't turn his head in her direction. "Much as I want to. I'm not following you into your house, either. Too tempting."

"I hadn't thought of that."

"Me, either." He stepped back and dug her key out of his pocket. "At first I took your suggestion and unlocked the door so I could wait inside. But the minute I walked in I started wondering if you'd kept the lantern lights up. I loved those things."

"I left them up."

"Ah. Well, I hotfooted it back out of your house before I got wound up."

"Smart."

"Which makes me think maybe you should take them down."

"But you like them."

"That's my point. Taking them down would be a good de-escalation move."

"I guess it would, but we don't have to rush into it. We can leave them up a little while longer."

"Well, good, then. I'll have that to look forward to after my next shift at the Buffalo."

And she could hardly wait to get him back in her bed. But they had an event to attend. "Um, we should probably—"

"Right, right. Listen, since you don't need money for anything, want to leave your wallet and just take this key?"

"Good idea." She grabbed her purse from the passenger seat and climbed out.

"Here you go." He handed it over.

The key was warm from resting in his pocket. Even that small detail set her on fire. "I'll also take my phone in case my mom needs to get in touch with me."

"Of course." His gaze swept over her and he swallowed. "I hope you can talk me down on the drive to the ranch. I've been thinking about you all day."

"I've been thinking about you, too."

"Nice to hear, but it doesn't help." He shoved his hands in his pockets as he walked with her back to the porch.

"Sorry I don't have any porch furniture you can sit on. I used to but I got rid of the old stuff and haven't replaced it yet."

"No worries. The steps are fine."

"I won't be long. I just need to change clothes."

"Take your time. I'll be out here not thinking about you changing your clothes."

"And I'll be in there changing clothes not thinking about you sitting out here not thinking about me."

"You'd better get going before the whole schedule collapses."

"Yep." She hurried up the steps. "See you in five."

Moments later she tossed her work clothes in the hamper and returned to her bedroom to take a quick glance in her full-length mirror. She'd chosen the outfit with his parents in mind. She wanted to project an image of a wholesome, caring person who'd be a good mom for their first grandchild.

Her new jeans fit well but weren't too tight. Her boots looked cute but not flashy and her paisley knit top in shades of blue had a girl-next-door vibe. Folks rarely dressed up at Rowdy Ranch, so she'd also be event-appropriate.

Even the wedding invitation had suggested wearing casual clothes. But she'd attended enough gatherings out there to know a little bling never hurt. The denim jacket and jeans she'd packed for the wedding sparkled a bit. But they weren't overtly sexy, either.

She brushed her hair and her teeth. A quick refresh of her makeup and she was ready to head out the door with her small suitcase.

For the overnight part of the visit she'd tucked in sweats. She'd never cared for filmy negligees and in this case alluring nightwear would be like throwing a match on a bonfire.

Taking her phone, she left her purse on its hook by the door, pocketed her key and walked out on the porch. "Ready."

He stood and turned around. "You look great."

"Not too sexy?"

"You're asking the wrong guy." He stepped up on the porch. "Let me take that."

"Thank you." She didn't quibble. Since he'd been eager to pick her up, naturally he'd want to carry her suitcase even if it wasn't heavy.

"Did you bring a hat?"

"No. Thought about it, but the one I have is old and faded. Not classy enough for a wedding and I assume we won't be going riding."

"No. But I volunteered us to help set up for the ceremony."

"I'll be okay."

"And if not, there are straw hats in the barn if you need one." He handed her into the truck before stowing her suitcase in the back seat.

She hadn't ridden in it since Tuesday night and the moment her tush settled into that plush seat, she was turned on by flashbacks.

He swung up behind the wheel and laid his hat on the dash before closing the door and buckling up. "Off we go." He turned the key in the ignition. The engine rumbled but the radio was silent.

"No music?"

"I couldn't handle it on the way in. Made me want to do things we don't have time for. But if you—"

"Let's leave it off. I don't need the extra stimulation, either. Just sitting in your cab gets me hot."

"Don't tell me that." He pulled away from the curb. "Although Rance would love to know he was right. He promised me this truck would increase my odds with the ladies."

"Has it?"

"Evidently. I've only tested it once and I'm batting a thousand."

"It's just been me?"

"So far it's a one-woman truck."

"Didn't your mom ride in it yesterday?"

"She did, but Rance wasn't referring to mothers when he said that. Plus Mom and Dad chose to sit in the back, so you're the only one who's ridden shotgun with me."

"Huh. So what did Rance have to say last night?"

"That I should stick with our plan."

"Does he think it'll work?"

"No."

"Do you?"

"Ask me again on Sunday morning. I'll have more information."

"Why?"

"We're about to be surrounded by a whole bunch of people. We haven't experienced that. Except for your mom at lunch and Dallas and Angie last night, it's just been us."

"Do crowds bother you?"

"No, but weddings do. I found that out at my brother's. I probably should warn you about that. I'll do my best to shake it off."

"Is that why you invited me for the weekend? To help you through it?"

He smiled, putting a crease in his freshly shaved cheek. "No, ma'am. I invited you because you'd be coming out for the wedding and I wanted to make sure you'd stay and spend the night with me. Then I decided I might as well go for two nights."

"But I can also be your support buddy if you start freaking out."

"I didn't freak out at Dallas's I just got very depressed. The vows were similar to the ones in my ceremony, and I hated hearing them. They sounded so fake. So hollow."

"I can imagine."

"How about you? Do those words upset you at all?"

"Not really. They don't make me either happy or sad because I don't picture myself standing at the altar hearing them. But you did. You believed in those words and then everything fell apart. That has to be worse."

"Don't feel too sorry for me. This time I'll be concentrating on how good it will feel once I'm lying in bed with you."

"Won't that be a risk for your easily excited friend?"

"Meaning you? Or my—"

"Both. When you get a certain look in your eye, I'm toast."

"You don't have to do a damn thing and I'm toast. I hear you catch your breath on the phone and I'm ready to make a thirty-minute drive." He sighed. "And we need to find a different topic."

"Your parents?"

"That'll do it."

"Did you spend time together today?"

"Sure did. Dallas, Angie and I took them riding again. We went yesterday and they wanted to go again."

"I didn't know they were riders."

"They weren't back in February. They struggled to stay on. But they've been taking lessons so it's more fun for them now."

"That's awesome."

"I think so, since Dallas and I are settled in for the duration. I think they're becoming attached to this place. Evidently they get a kick out of sleeping in the kids' wing of the ranch house. They like the rustic atmosphere."

"I think I'm gonna enjoy your parents."

"They'll enjoy you, too. If we'd only move in together, they'd be totally pleased with the situation."

"Will my coming out to spend the next two nights with you give them false hope?"

"Yes, it will."

"Should I try to make a case for our plan of action? Or rather, eventual inaction?"

"That depends on whether you'd be comfortable explaining how we're going to wean ourselves off an activity we obviously enjoy."

And oh, did she ever enjoy it. His comment was enough to heat her up again. Maybe talking about her mom would cool things down. "I told my mother about the new plan this morning."

"How did that go?"

"She didn't buy it."

"Neither will my folks."

"Probably not. And since I'm not wild about the idea of discussing it with them, I'll just keep my mouth shut."

"I think that's for the best."

And she was out of distractions and back to being extremely aware of the yummy man within easy reach. She longed to give his denim-clad thigh a squeeze. Not a good idea.

His chest heaved and he kept his gaze on the road. "I know what you're thinking about."

"No, you don't."

"Do so. Your breathing changed and you're shifting around in your seat."

"It's this truck. It makes me remember the first night and then Tuesday night and then—"

"Want me to sell it?"

"Sell it? Why in the world would you do that?"

"Then I could buy something boring that doesn't turn you on. Seems like a logical solution to the problem and would help the cause."

"No! You love this truck. I would never want you to sell it because I have a problem. I'll deal with it. Put that crazy idea right out of your head."

"Okay, but I would do it if that moves us closer to the goal."

"That's very noble of you, but we'll find some other way to deescalate the situation."

"Let me know what you come up with."

"I will." But at the moment, deescalating was the last thing on her mind.

33

Rance was effing brilliant. Trent planned to tell him so the minute he had a chance. He'd come up with a strategy to test whether Brittany really wanted to dial it back or only thought she did.

Risk was involved. The lantern lights were no big deal, but if she'd wanted him to sell his truck, he would have had to do it. He'd counted on her rejection of the concept because she clearly liked riding in it.

If that turned her on, so what? Their strong mutual attraction could be viewed as a gift and not a problem to be eliminated.

Maybe eventually she'd realize that. He didn't mind the separate living quarters idea, although he wished they were geographically closer. Right next door would be good.

But why give up lovemaking when they found it so satisfying? If they were clear that they weren't looking for a happily ever after, everything would be fine. The baby would be fine, too.

"We still have thirty minutes before we need to be at the ranch house, so I planned to stop at my cabin so we can drop off your suitcase."

"That's fine."

"And I can give you something I picked up today. It's a late birthday present and an early Mother's Day present."

"Oh, Trent, you didn't have to—"

"I wanted to. It'll come in handy this weekend."

"Where is it?" She scooted around in her seat. "I don't see anything. Is it tiny?"

"Not so tiny. I used your suitcase to keep it hidden so I can surprise you."

Settling back, she gave him a smile. "That's very nice. Surprises are fun."

"I hope you like it." He pulled up to his cabin. After Dallas's comment about the porch swing, he'd found himself looking at that swing a lot. And arguing with Dallas in his head.

Shutting off the engine, he pointed to it. "I should give you that."

She frowned. "No, you shouldn't. What's up with you? First you want to sell your truck and now you're trying to give me your porch swing."

"I can't picture sitting in it by myself and it's not long enough for me to lie down. But you could lie in it, and once the baby comes, you could rock her to sleep."

"I'm not taking your swing. Even if you don't use it much, it looks great there. Cozy."

And that was the point. Once upon a time he'd wanted cozy, thought he'd achieved it, and his world had come apart like a poorly designed bird's nest.

If Dallas was right, and buying that swing was a subconscious effort to rebuild that nest, he needed to get rid of it ASAP and keep an eye on those tendencies. "But you don't have any porch furniture."

"I'll buy some, the collapsible kind that I can easily take with me when I move."

"Move?" His attention shifted immediately. "You're moving?"

"Not right away, but I'll need a backyard that's safe for her to run around in. My current one won't work and I'm not putting time and money into a rental."

"A yard. I didn't think of that." He gazed at his cabin. He could fence in an area outside the back door and build a swing set himself rather than buy the ready-made kind. How about a sandbox? Yeah, he'd—

"Trent?"

"What?" He blinked. "Sorry. I was busy putting together Montana's backyard." Hm. Should he be worried about his eagerness to do that? Maybe.

"She'll love it here. And by the way, *you* can rock her on that swing, so don't go giving it away."

"All right, I won't." He climbed out of the truck. "Stay put, please, and don't turn around. I'll fetch your surprise."

Opening the back door on his side, he nudged her suitcase out of the way and pulled out the rounded box. If she'd been able to see it, she'd have guessed immediately.

He walked around the back of the truck and opened her door. "Happy birthday and happy Mom's Day."

"A hat?" Her face lit up just the way he'd hoped. She popped off the lid and gasped. "It's a silverbelly!"

"That's what they called it at Hannigan's. When I mentioned I was looking for a gift for you and was leaning toward a hat, a lady took me right to this one. She said you come in every so often and try it on."

"I do! But it's so expens—"

"Like I said, it covers two occasions." Happiness swelled in his chest. "Let me have the box so you can come on down and put on the hat."

She handed it to him and scrambled out. "I can't believe you got me this. I've been in love with it for months, but I couldn't bring myself to spend the money since I have my old black one."

"The woman at Hannigan's said this gray mist color will go with your hair…." He trailed off as she put it on and faced him. "Wow."

"Good?"

"Beautiful."

"It's a gorgeous hat."

"I'm not talking about the hat."

She gazed up at him, her blue eyes warm. "You're very sweet to say that. And so generous."

"You're welcome. And bonus, when you're wearing it, kissing you won't be so easy."

"That's what you think." Nudging back her hat, she rose on tiptoe, slid her hand behind his head, and pulled him close. "Thank you for this amazing gift."

He closed his eyes and savored the velvet touch of her mouth, the flavor of peppermint toothpaste on her tongue, and the press of her fingers against his scalp. Knowing he shouldn't, he gathered her close, relishing the warmth of her body and the glorious sensation as he tightened his hold and she melted into him.

It took all his will power to put a tiny space between her lips and his. "We can't do this."

"I know." She swallowed. "I'll count to three and we'll both let go."

"Okay."

"One, two, three."

He turned her loose and she backed away, her breathing as wonky as his. He cleared his throat. "If one hat doesn't stop us from kissing, I'll bet two hats will."

"It's more complicated with two."

"I'll wear mine, then." He paused. "Except that makes me sexier. While I'm inside I'll grab my baseball cap." Rance would be proud of him for that idea.

She made a face and tugged down the brim of her Stetson. "No."

Adorable. "Just trying to help."

"I understand that, but please don't ditch your hat. It suits you."

"That gray one sure suits you." He gestured toward the cabin. "Door's unlocked. Go check it out in the bathroom mirror. I'll get your suitcase."

"Thanks." She flashed him a smile and started toward the porch.

He watched her walk away, partly because he loved how she moved and partly because she looked so damn cute wearing the hat he'd bought her. Seeing it on her made his heart beat faster and his breath catch. His chest warmed and tickled, like he had fuzz balls in there....

Aw, *hell*. Dammit to *hell*. Dallas was right about the swing, about second chances, about everything. There was a big fat, flashing-neon-lights reason why he'd bought her that hat.

He was in love with her. And she would hate it, but she needed to know.

34

It's only a hat. Brit kept telling herself that as she admired it in his bathroom mirror. But it wasn't just a hat, was it?

Trent had taken the time to find her something special. Not a trinket or a bouquet of flowers that would die in a week, but something she would cherish and wear for years.

Her focus on his hat last Saturday night might have inspired him to get her a really nice one. Or he'd made a lucky guess and nailed it. Or maybe, just maybe, he'd paid close attention.

They'd made love and shared breakfast in her modest rented house where no luxury items were in evidence. He'd seen the low-budget truck she drove. An observant person would figure out she was unlikely to treat herself to a pricey Stetson when something cheaper would do the job.

His choice of a gift impressed the hell out of her. It also made her a little nervous, as if it had significance. Nah, it was just a *hat*. She was overthinking it.

The soft thud of her suitcase on the wooden floor brought her out of the bathroom and face-to-face with her thoughtful lover. "It's a fabulous hat. You couldn't have given me a more... what's wrong?" She gazed in confusion at his stony expression.

"I need to tell you something and you're not going to like it. But it's only fair for me to—"

"What? What's happened?"

He sucked in a breath and glanced around. "Let's go in the living room." Turning on his heel, he walked out the door.

She hurried after him, her heart slamming against her ribs. "Good grief? Did you get a phone call? Is someone in serious trouble?"

"Not someone, but some*thing*." He turned back to her. "Dallas kept telling me I was fooling myself, but I wanted to believe he was wrong."

"About what?"

"About me." He scrubbed a hand through his hair. "He said I bought that swing because I secretly still want what I used to have, or thought I had, with Cheryl."

"You had a swing before?"

"No. It's the idea of it, two people in love getting cozy on a swing. You even said it looked cozy."

Her stomach began to churn. "Go on."

"I told Dallas he was nuts, that I was not taking that chance ever again, but now I realize...I'm so sorry, Brittany. I promised you I wouldn't—"

"Don't you dare ask me to marry—"

"I won't! But this is just as bad, maybe worse." His gaze locked with hers. "I'm in love with you."

Her brain refused to process the words. Then she finally did. "No, you're not. It's just—"

"Yes, I am. I've been here before and I know what it feels like. I should have recognized the signs but I didn't want to admit that I—"

"You honestly think you're in love with me?"

"I know I am."

"You can't be." She clasped her hands in front of her to control the shaking. "Not in the space of a week. It's because we've had this incredible physical—"

"That's what I told myself, but it was never true, not even in the beginning."

"Come on. We were virtual strangers that first night."

"Not for long. I've been pretending it wasn't happening, but I can't ignore it anymore. Just now, when I watched you going into the house, it hit me, and I knew without a shadow of a doubt."

The shaking got worse. Maybe it didn't matter whether he was actually in love with her. If he believed he was, that was just as bad. "I'm sure it's temporary, like a crush."

"I'm sure it's not."

"When did you buy that swing?"

"Last week."

"So it was before we got together on Saturday night. That means it has nothing to do with me, or with us. Your brother could be totally wrong about that swing."

"But what if he's right about my state of mind when I chose it? What if it's the first crack in my resistance to getting—"

"I think you're overreacting. Of course you like me a lot after what we've shared. I like you a lot, too. I was overcome with tender emotion because you bought me this hat, which is why I kissed you. That doesn't mean I'm in love with you."

"What if I bought it because I'm in love with you?"

That hit a nerve. Her breath hitched. A man who was falling in love would pay attention. He would seek out the perfect gift. But could love really happen in a *week*?

"You're starting to believe me. I can see it in your eyes."

"I believe you think you're in love. But be logical. We met seven days ago."

"You can't use logic in our situation. It's not like we've been casually dating for a week."

"No, but—"

"Look, I'm not happy about this. I considered not telling you until later, but if I'd waited, I'd find more reasons not to tell you. For instance, I couldn't tell you when we were in bed."

"Why not?"

"Because you'd think it was because of what happened in that bed. This goes way beyond sex. And it'll get worse."

"Worse?"

"In terms of messing up our plan."

"So what do you want to do?"

"I don't know." He checked his phone. "And we don't have time to figure it out. The rehearsal starts in fifteen minutes and you haven't been reintroduced to my parents yet, so I'm sure they're hoping we'll—"

"Let's go. We'll put this subject aside for now and talk about it when we get back here."

"Then we're off."

They rode in silence the short distance to the ranch house. But there was nothing quiet about what was going on in her head.

She'd kept her hat on, an advantage of being short. But it meant she had to tilt her head a little to check on Trent, the beautiful man who'd just declared his love for her.

He gave new meaning to the phrase *jaw carved from granite.* He stared straight ahead, at least whenever she glanced over there.

I'm in love with you. That couldn't be true, could it? She replayed the moment when he'd told her, the intensity in his brown eyes mirroring the emotion in his voice. She'd tried not to hear it.

But now she couldn't hear anything else. It wasn't the first time a man had said he loved her, but it was the most potent because he'd had the courage to confess something he knew she didn't want to hear.

It gave a different meaning to their passionate encounters. Those probably should end now. It was the kind thing to do. Continuing under these circumstances would be selfish of her.

The thought of no longer sharing that joy with him made her ache, and he would suffer at least as much if not more. Sure, they'd intended to give it up eventually, just not this soon. But he needed to fall out of love with her.

When Trent rounded the curve, giving her a view of the house, she sucked in a breath. This would be tricky. The crowd gathered on the porch and in the yard was filled with familiar faces. Except for his parents and a few others, she'd known these folks all her life.

The McLintock clan now included spouses and in some cases the parents or grandparents of those spouses. Mrs. J, B&B owner and Molly's grandmother, would be here, along with Liz and Gerald Bradley, Ella and Faye's parents.

Ella. Brit prayed her best friend would understand why she hadn't been informed early on. And forgive her for holding back the news.

Trent beeped the horn as he drove past the house and headed for the tractor barn where a new and much larger parking area had been marked off.

The house had become the backdrop for the ceremony. A greenery-covered arch at the top of the porch steps would likely be the altar. In the front yard, four rows of temporary benches made of planks and cinderblocks provided seating with an aisle in between.

"That's a cool idea for the seating, but that's not enough benches, is it?"

"No. We're putting up the rest in the morning." Trent eased into a parking space next to Midnight Thunder, Rance's big black truck. At least fifteen others were there, too, along with a couple of SUVs.

"This won't hold all the vehicles, though."

"This one's for the wedding party. We passed the spot for the guest one, which is right before you round the curve." He switched off the motor.

"I couldn't imagine how they'd handle such a huge crowd, but it seems like they've got it covered."

"We do."

She picked up on his subtle correction. She'd used *they* and he'd changed it to *we*. He considered himself part of Rowdy Ranch, now.

Movement in her sideview mirror caught her attention. "I think your parents are on their way over." Vanessa's chin-length hair was still brown and Harry hadn't covered his silver. Their picture-perfect Western wear marked them as greenhorns, but the effort was endearing.

Trent checked his rearview. "Yep. That's why I beeped, although I'm sure they saw us drive in."

"Don't bother helping me out." She opened her door. "We don't have time to stand on ceremony."

"No, ma'am. Meet you at the tailgate." Grabbing his hat, he climbed down.

Her throat tight and her pulse racing, she left the truck to meet two people who would willingly die for the man whose heart she held in her hands.

_35_

Trent pasted a smile on his face as his mom and dad hurried toward him.

"I'm so glad you're here," his mother said. "We were about to give up on you."

"Sorry. We ran a little behind." As Brittany came around the back fender, he held out his arm. "Here she is. Brittany, come meet Vanessa and Harry, although I think you might've bumped into each other in February." He drew her into a side hug before turning her loose so she could shake hands with his parents.

"Of course we did." His mother abandoned the handshake routine and gave Brittany a quick embrace. "It's great to see you again. Nice hat."

"Thank you." She flushed and glanced at him. "Trent gave it to me."

His mom added a nod of approval. "Nice work, son."

His dad stepped forward and hugged her briefly. "Welcome to the family, Brittany."

Trent winced at the phrase, but she took it in stride, thanking him with a smile.

"Is it Brittany? Or Brit?" His mom's tone was chipper, the one she used to get through awkward moments.

"I answer to both."

"Well, I agree with Trent. Brittany is a lovely name. Both our girls shortened theirs. I wish they'd been able to come, but Sara couldn't leave work and one of Lani's best friends is getting married this weekend. They'll be with us for the August trip. They're eager to get back out here."

Trent would just bet they were. They'd been shooting him texts all day. He'd answered about half of them. Some, like Sara's *What the hell, Trent?* didn't require one.

He was damned lucky they hadn't come on this trip. They would have thrown themselves into his mess in a heartbeat. He'd have it sorted out by August. Most likely by tomorrow morning.

At least Brittany hadn't blown up when he'd told her. That wouldn't have been her style, but then again, he'd never given her reason to pitch a fit.

On the drive over he'd questioned the wisdom of his timing, but now he could see he'd done the right thing. She'd have several hours when they couldn't talk, hours when she could let his confession percolate. He'd do the same. Tonight they'd work it out.

Someone over by the house yelled *time to start.* Trent's money was on Sky. As the oldest, he usually marshalled the troops like Dallas used to do when they'd all lived at home.

Trent held out a hand to Brittany. "We'd better get over there. Don't want to miss anything."

"No, we don't." She slid her fingers through his without hesitation and squeezed.

It was a simple thing, but it made his heart stutter. Nothing about this relationship was simple.

"Desiree keeps protesting they don't need a rehearsal," his mom said as she and his dad walked with them back toward the crowd. "But with all the people in this wedding, I think they do."

Brit surveyed the large group. "How many are in it?"

"A lot," his dad said. "The bulk of who's standing there."

Nobody in the boisterous crowd had paid them any attention, which suited Trent just fine. He paused before they reached the benches and the knot of people clustered near the porch steps. "Since we're not part of it, let's hang out here for a minute, let them get organized."

"Sure." His mom turned back toward him. So did his dad.

With his folks providing a screen for Brittany, he tugged her close to his side. "Are we supposed to sit in a certain spot?"

"I asked that," his mom said. "Usually these benches would be for the groom's family and friends and the other side would be for the bride's. But everybody's connected to both of them, so we can sit wherever we—"

"Brit?"

Trent braced himself as Ella broke away from the group and rushed over. Let the games begin.

"Brit Powers, you're a sneaky one!" Ella's attention darted over to him, down to their linked hands and back up to Brittany's face. "When did—"

"We need to talk." She kept her voice low. "I'll find you later."

"Don't worry. I'll find *you*, girlfriend." Ella laughed and hurried back to Marsh. Evidently she said something to him, because he looked over at Trent and gave him a thumbs up.

The news rippled through the group like a crowd doing the wave as heads turned in his direction. He sighed as the McLintock gang exchanged smiles and fist bumps.

Brittany rose up on her toes. "What's happening?"

"The news is out and they're happy for me. For *us*, too, of course, but mostly for me."

His mother leaned close. "I'm lost. What news is out? I thought only—"

"Just Desiree, Andy, Dallas and Angie." He kept his head down and his voice soft. "Oh, and Rance as of last night. That's it."

"So why are they making such a big deal of you bringing a date to the rehearsal?"

Brittany's fingers tightened in silent support.

"Because I haven't gone out with anyone since I moved here."

"First of all, why not, and second of all, how do they know you haven't been dating?"

He chose to answer the easy one first. "Because that's how it works in this family. They keep an eye on things, make sure everyone's doing okay."

"And you've been sitting alone in your cabin since January?"

"Not at all. Something's always going on here. Then Rance got me the bartending gig. I've been fine, Mom."

"They're ready to go, son." His dad gestured toward the wedding party, which had moved to the far side of the yard and lined up in order. Music from a boom box began playing and the minister had taken his position on the porch. "We should sit."

Trent glanced at the handful of people who weren't part of the ceremony. They were all in the front row of the bride's side. Nobody had taken the front row of the groom's side, maybe because he, his folks and Brittany had been standing close to it. He looked down at her. "You okay sitting right here?"

"Sure, why not?"

He kept hold of her as they turned around and sat on the smooth wooden plank.

His mom tucked in on his left side. "I understand getting acclimated before you jump back in, but—"

"I never intended to jump back in."

"You never told me that."

"Because I knew you wouldn't like it."

"You weren't going to date at all?"

"That's right."

"Then I'm really glad Brit changed your mind."

"Mm." Brittany hadn't just changed his mind. She'd blown it to smithereens.

36

Ella didn't make good on her promise to find Brit after the rehearsal or during the chaotic rehearsal dinner in Rowdy Roost. No surprise there.

The McLintocks were in rare form as they celebrated their mother's upcoming marriage. Nobody sat down, not even when they ate, and the small dance floor was packed with ever-changing partners.

At one point Beau moved through the crowd cutting in and dancing with each of his brothers plus Andy. That inspired Rance to do the same. Then Angie announced her intention to dance with each of the women.

Fortunately Brit had learned years ago how to dance in a hat. She swung from bouts of joyful laughter as she threw herself into the fray, and moments of sickening dread whenever she caught a glimpse of Trent. How the hell could they work through this?

Maybe Ella would have some advice. They'd known each other since kindergarten, so if anyone could help her, Ella would be the one. She also knew Trent, at least a little.

As the party started winding down, she finally had her opportunity. Ella dashed through the swinging doors alone. Brit recognized that behavior because she was doing it more lately.

She followed Ella out and raced after her. "Ella!"

"Brit!" She spun around. "I want to talk but I need to—"

"Go ahead. I'll wait outside the door."

"Got it." She barreled into the small bathroom at the end of the hall.

Leaning against the wall, Brit ran through what she needed to tell her, cutting out any unimportant details. They wouldn't have much time.

Ella opened the door. "Let's go to the library." She headed off, her long legs eating up the distance.

Brit had to trot to keep up with her, but she didn't ask her to slow down. This was normal behavior for a long-legged basketball star and a short-legged gymnast.

Once they were inside, Brit closed the door, took a deep breath and talked fast.

Ella listened, her expression changing from smiling indulgence to wide-eyed amazement.

Finally Brit came to the last reveal. She sucked in more air. "And this afternoon, right before we drove over here, he said he's in love with me."

"Holy shit."

"He's gotta be confusing good sex with love. He says he's not, that what he's experiencing is different, bigger. But it's been seven days. *Seven days,* Ella."

"True, but..." She pointed to the silverbelly Stetson, which hadn't left Brit's head since she'd first put it on. "Whether he's in love with you or not, he's tuned into you, unless you accidentally told him about that hat."

"I did not. I complimented him on his hat but I didn't say a word about wanting a new one myself, let alone this one."

Ella gazed at her. "I'm not at all surprised that he figured out the perfect gift for you. That fits what I know about him. He's a good guy, Brit."

"I didn't say he wasn't, but I'm the first woman he's been with since his ex. He was divorced only six months ago. And he's supposedly in love with me after only a week? I'd be a fool to believe that's possible."

"I do have some more info for you. When I saw you two together before the rehearsal I asked Marsh if he knew when Trent left his cheating ex. It's been almost eighteen months since he walked out."

"It took a year to finalize it?"

"Because she tried every legal trick in the book to get more money out of him."

"Did she succeed?"

"He finally agreed to give her more to get it over with."

"Is he broke?"

Ella laughed. "Does it matter?"

"No! I just hate the idea that she might have left him with virtually nothing. He's so generous and I would hate to think he couldn't afford this hat."

"He can afford the hat. And he is generous, with his time and his money. We've all seen that. But Marsh says he's also... what word did he use? Cautious. Marsh says he's cautious."

"Really? Because that's not the word I'd use to describe him. A cautious man wouldn't have agreed to father this child. And he definitely wouldn't have announced he'd fallen in love after only seven days."

"Unless he was smitten with you from the beginning."

That rang a bell. He had said something like that. "But he agreed to the original plan to have this baby, live separately, and be friends, not lovers. If he was into me, why would he say yes to that idea?"

"Okay, ask yourself that question." Ella smiled. "See what you come up with."

"That something was better than nothing, and maybe the agreement would change?"

"Bingo."

"I don't think he told himself that. I do think he expected the process would take longer."

"Was he happy when it didn't?"

"No. Neither was I. So I came up with a different plan."

"The gradual weaning off plan?" Ella looked amused.

"It could have worked, damn it. Remember my diet soda program?"

"Oh, yeah. But sex isn't soda."

"Whatever. Doesn't matter if it would have worked. We're way past that. Although I thought he was good with it. Today he offered suggestions for ways to help us cut back, but then... the hat and *I love you*."

Ella was silent for a moment. "Okay, what if, against all odds, he's telling the truth? What if he's madly in love with you? How would you feel about it?"

She met Ella's warm gaze. "Petrified."

37

Trent watched Brittany tear after Ella. When neither of them came back right away, he figured they'd escaped to a private location to talk about him.

He sipped on his unleaded beer and checked his phone. His parents had already retreated to their room. The volume on the music had been reduced from fire siren level to loud. Might be time to hit the road.

A hand on his shoulder made him turn.

Marsh stood there, a sympathetic gleam in his eyes. "It's an uneasy feeling when they go off to talk about you and you don't know whether the discussion will go in your favor or not."

"I suppose you would have experienced that."

"Yeah, but don't worry. Ella thinks a lot of you. We both do. She'll put in a good word."

"I appreciate it." He smiled. "I could use one or two of those."

"Nice job getting Brit the hat she's been pining over."

"She told you I bought it?"

"Ella and I asked. She's wanted it for months. Ella and Faye considered getting it for her birthday, but even splitting the cost in half would be way more than the three of them usually spend on each other. They didn't want to up the ante and make her think she should find something in that range when it was their turn."

"Whereas for me, the sky's the limit."

Marsh chuckled. "I know that impulse. And bonus, she loves the hat."

"She seems to."

"It makes sense that you two would find each other. Neither of you wants a commitment right now."

"Right." He hesitated. He wouldn't reveal anything about the baby, not when the wedding was less than twenty-four hours away. But Marsh had known Brittany a long time. "I might have screwed things up."

"Already? I thought you just got together."

"We did, and I know it's not supposed to work this way, but... I'm in love with her."

Marsh frowned. "I hate to say it, dude, but if she's your first after a long dry spell, that could feel like—"

"I told myself that. But from the very beginning, something about her clicked and locked right into place. That feeling just gets stronger by the day. By the minute, even. I didn't feel that with Cheryl. Or any woman I've been with."

"I can't argue with that. Not my experience, but I suppose it can happen. I wouldn't tell her, though. Not yet."

"Too late."

"Well, damn. No wonder she chased after Ella."

"It seemed really important to let her know."

"You spooked her. She's brave about most things, but not a relationship with a guy."

"Because of her parents splitting."

He nodded. "Fifth grade. We were at recess when she told us. She's always been small compared to Ella and me. But that day she was so tiny."

His gut clenched. "I hate that she went through that."

"If you ask me, she never got over it. She wants kids, but no guy ever measures up. She's afraid to trust them." Marsh glanced past him. "They just came back."

"I need to talk with her. I'll see if she's ready to leave."

"Good luck."

"Thanks." He walked toward Ella and Brittany. "Have a good chat?"

Ella smiled. "Absolutely. How about you and Marsh? Did you solve all the problems of the world?"

"Not quite." He glanced at Brittany. "My folks left the party a little while ago. They said to tell you they'd see you tomorrow for the bench-building party."

"We're doing that, too," Ella said. "I'm gonna find Marsh and drag him out of here. Tomorrow's a big day." She turned to Brittany and hugged her. "See you then."

"You bet. G'night."

"Are you ready to go, too?"

She turned and met his gaze. "Yes. Yes, I am."

He longed to read passion in those blue eyes. Instead he saw only firm resolve. "Then let's say our goodbyes and leave."

It took a while to accomplish that, and he had to endure the winks and knowing looks from people who thought he and Brittany were going back to his cabin for a roll in the hay. He figured his chances were slim to none.

Because his chest hurt like hell, he decided to open the dialogue as soon as they started the walk to the truck. "Do you want to talk now or wait until we're at the cabin?"

"We can wait."

"Just so you know, if you'd like me to take you back home tonight, I will."

"That's good to know. Thank you."

Knowing that could happen increased the pressure in his chest. Although if they were ending things, wouldn't it be better to just do it?

No, it wouldn't. If she'd give him one more night, he'd take it.

He helped her into the truck because he was looking for every excuse to touch her. He might not have many more of those.

Making small talk had never been a talent of his, so he didn't try on the way back to the cabin. When they got there, he helped her back out and kept holding her hand as he shut the door.

She didn't try to pull away, but she didn't weave her fingers through his like she had when they'd been talking with his parents. It was a small difference, but it registered.

He kept holding her hand as they climbed the steps, crossed the porch and walked inside. He had the living room lamps on either side of the sofa on a timer, so the room looked welcoming.

But maybe not welcoming enough to make a difference. He wanted her to like walking into his cabin, to imagine herself doing it every day when she came home from work.

Oh, yeah, his subconscious had been busy ever since she'd mentioned that she'd have to move to somewhere with a yard for Montana. If she had to move, why not live in his cabin, where there would be a yard as soon as he bought some building materials?

He cleared his throat. "Want to talk here?"

"Sure." She started pacing.

"Want something to drink?

"No, thanks."

"Want to sit?"

She shook her head and continued to pace, not meeting his gaze. "The thing is, I have trouble believing in true love to begin with, let alone a love that springs up out of nowhere in a few days. We can't even count Sunday and Monday. Tuesday was almost over by the time I walked to the Buffalo."

"And I wish I could say I've reconsidered. But I can't. I love you."

She finally looked at him, misery in her blue eyes. "Why? How? You barely know me!"

"I know you care about others, including me, or you wouldn't be so torn up about this. You'd laugh at me and demand to be taken home."

"I don't know anybody who would be that mean."

"I do. Being married to someone exactly that mean and then meeting you is like being taken from darkness to light. You didn't manipulate me into the baby thing. You gave me time to decide. And now I know why I did."

"Because of the sex?"

"No, dammit! Because I watched you acting like a kid on that barstool and that's when I fell for you. Before we climbed in my truck and I realized you wanted me."

"The spinning barstool?"

"Do you know how many people in this world have forgotten how to be silly? Cheryl almost turned me into one of them. And suddenly there you were with the Happy Birthday song set to go off at the moment you were born, proud of being a year older."

"Except worried. I've read the stats on pregnancies."

"Because you don't have your head in the sand. Your concern is valid. So what do you do? Marry someone just to get a baby? No, you're not capable of that. Instead you come up with a creative plan which benefits someone besides just you."

"So I'm a decent person who likes to spin on barstools. That hardly seems like enough to—"

"Are you fishing?"

"No! I just—"

"You're gutsy. Asking me was a bold move. Talking to Desiree took nerve. You also listened and revised your plan as a result. You're flexible."

"Duh. I was a gymnast."

"I didn't mean physically, although your body drives me—"

"See? That's—"

"But it's not the main draw! You know what? We could try an experiment. But first let me know — have you decided whether I'm taking you home tonight?"

"It would probably be easier on both of us if you did."

"Or you could give me a chance to prove I can spend the rest of the night in bed with you and all we'll do is sleep."

"You can't do it."

"Try me."

38

Despite herself, Brit was intrigued. She knew firsthand how much he craved her. "It's an interesting idea."

"There will be ground rules. You can't try to seduce me. If you do, all bets are off."

"I promise I won't. Will we cuddle?"

"I might not be that strong. But we can hold hands."

"Will we wear anything?"

"I'll put on my sweats. What did you bring?"

"Nothing."

He groaned. "Should've guessed."

"I have sweats and a sweatshirt. But I hate sleeping in them. Too hot and bulky."

"Underwear?"

"Too binding. Want to call it off?"

"No, dammit. I won't wear my sweats, either. It'll be the ultimate test. Are you in?"

"It's a nutty idea."

"But you like those."

"I do." She gazed at him. "I can't believe you got hooked on me because I wanted to spin on those stools. I thought you'd find it annoying."

"Which means you need to learn more about me."

"Could be." She flashed back to the moment when she and Angie had come into the cabin to find the two brothers playing keep-away by the kitchen door.

"Are you in?"

"I'm in. Just so I don't sabotage you in the first two minutes, I'll go in first and call you when I'm under the covers."

"That's kind of you."

"I'm outta here." She left at a brisk walk, careful not to sway her hips. He wouldn't make it through the night. But if he didn't, her conscience would be clear.

She made it through her bedtime routine quickly and slipped into bed, the sheets cool and smooth against her body. No doubt he'd put on fresh ones this morning.

Turning toward the wall, she pulled the covers up to her neck. "Okay, Trent! You're up!" Then she giggled. "Sorry."

"Sure you are." His boots clicked on the wooden floor.

She stifled another giggle and controlled the urge to roll over and look at him. The sounds of him undressing electrified her naked body. When he brushed his teeth, she could taste his kisses. Would she be the one to crack?

The click of the bathroom light going off and his footsteps on the wood floor sent her pulse into hyperdrive. The mattress shivered as he climbed in. So did she.

"Lights out." He switched off the one on his side.

She'd have to stretch to reach hers, baring her arm and shoulder. She should have thought of it earlier. "Don't look."

"I'm closing my eyes."

She snapped off the light, leaving them in darkness. Inches apart. Naked. Her skin flushed hot.

"How're you doing over there?"

"Fine." She rolled to her back.

"Me, too. Just dandy." His breathing didn't sound like he was fine.

She snickered. "Nobody says that anymore."

"What?"

"Dandy."

"Picked it up from Grandpa Elmer."

"Is he still around?"

"Going strong at ninety-two. Grandma Lily is ninety-one. Still water-skis."

"I hope Montana inherits those genes."

"I hope she gets your blue eyes."

"Brown works for me. Then I can sing her *Brown Eyed Girl*."

"You can sing?"

"No, I'm terrible, but she won't care."

"I'll bet you're not terrible. Sing some of it. That'll distract me."

"Oh, it'll distract you all right."

"Seriously. Do it."

"You'll be sorry, especially since I'm lying on my back, but if you insist." She launched into the song.

After the first couple of lines he started laughing.

She sang louder, which turned out to be awesome at releasing the tension of lying in bed with a naked and extremely accessible Trent Armstrong.

Eventually he was laughing so hard he was gasping for breath. "Okay, okay! You're the worst!"

She grinned. "Told you."

"Thank you. That helped."

"It was good for me, too."

"Wanna hold hands?"

"Sure."

"Slide your hand over, but do it slowly."

"Right. Don't want to touch something I shouldn't."

"Exactly." His breath hitched. "I feel the tips of your fingers."

"I feel yours." She slipped her hand over his palm.

He closed his fingers around it. "Sleep tight, Brittany."

"You, too, Trent." She concentrated on her breathing and the firm clasp of his hand.

Slowly her muscles relaxed. His presence was arousing, but comforting, too. His breathing evened out. So did hers. She drifted in and out.

The chirp of a bird penetrated a dream that involved barstools singing *Brown Eyed Girl.* Why was a bird chirping in the middle of the night?

Except it wasn't the middle of the night. Pale light filled the room. Trent's side of the bed was empty. He'd done it. Or had he?

Was he in the kitchen making coffee? Doubtful. She'd smell it brewing. Outside the birds were waking up, but inside nothing stirred.

She'd left her sweats and sweatshirt on the nightstand so she'd have something to wear when she woke up. Climbing out of bed, she put them on and went in search of Trent.

She found him on the sofa wearing his sweats. He'd draped the afghan over his bare chest and propped his head on one of the sofa's decorative pillows. He was sound asleep.

Easing down on the armchair, she settled in to wait. With his beard growing in and his long, dark lashes fanned over his flushed cheeks, he was a fascinating combination of rugged masculinity and beauty.

He'd tucked his bare feet under the other decorative pillow. The room was chilly and the green and yellow afghan barely covered his impressive torso. He needed another blanket.

Rising from the chair, she padded back into the bedroom, opened the closet and found one on the top shelf. Sage gazed up at her from her spot on the closet floor next to his boots.

Brit gave the bear a pat on the head before carrying the blanket into the living room. As she gently laid it over her sleeping prince, he woke up.

Lifting his head, he stared at her in confusion. Then he squeezed his eyes shut and let his head fall back. "I failed the test."

"How long did you last?"

"Maybe a couple of hours. Tried to sleep. Couldn't do it." He opened his eyes and gazed up at the beamed ceiling. "Then I focused on you singing *Brown Eyed Girl* because that was so damn funny."

"That didn't help? Because there's nothing sexy about me singing, especially that song. I murder it."

"You do." He scooted up. The blanket and afghan fell away as his chest heaved. "And you don't care. Which makes me love you all the more."

She gulped. "Trent, let's not—"

"Yeah, let's not get into that again. I know you don't want to hear it and my lame attempt to prove it fell apart." Tossing aside the afghan and blanket, he swung his long legs to the floor and stood.

"But you left the bed instead of waking me up. That's a partial victory."

"I suppose." He met her gaze. "But I'm through trying to prove it to you. Or anyone. The fact is I love everything about you — your bright spirit, your loyalty, your courage, and yes, your body. When I'm holding you I get all that, and it's the best gift I've ever been given. I love you, and if you don't believe me, there's nothing I can do about it."

39

Trent didn't have anything more to say, and evidently neither did Brittany. They exchanged very few words as they ate breakfast and got dressed. She'd brought some knockabout clothes for the ride home on Sunday and she wore those for the morning's work party.

She asked to borrow his baseball cap because she didn't want to risk getting the silverbelly dirty. She pulled her hair through the back. That cap had never looked so good.

He didn't ask her whether she'd leave after the reception or stick around. Since her mother would be driving out for the wedding, she had an option that didn't include him.

Good thing she had that choice. If she decided to end their physical relationship, he'd rather not endure the trip back to her house.

With Angie directing the bench assembly and many hands doing the job, they soon had enough rows to seat the multitude arriving for the five o'clock ceremony. Sam raced among the benches, his flag of a tail waving as he collected ear scratches and the occasional treat.

Brittany chose to work with Ella and Faye and he ended up with a group that included his folks and Marsh. When Marsh joined him for a water break and asked how things were going, he decided the guy had attached himself to that crew on purpose.

He wiped his forehead on his sleeve as he decided how to answer. "She still doesn't believe me. So I've let it go."

"You're giving up?"

"That's not an option." He'd be tied to her for the rest of his life, but Marsh didn't know that yet. "I've stopped trying to convince her, though."

Marsh nodded. "Smart."

"Don't know about smart, but it's calmed me down some." He glanced at Marsh. "Have you heard her sing *Brown Eyed Girl*?"

Marsh started to laugh. "Oh, no. Tell me she didn't."

"She did." The night hadn't been a success in any sense of the word, but remembering that part made him smile.

"Did you laugh? I hope you laughed."

"Couldn't help it."

"Good, because that's what she's going for. If you'd tried to pretend you liked it, you'd lose points." He nudged back his hat, his gaze steady. "She doesn't sing that song for just anybody. She has to trust you before she'll do it."

"Oh?"

"You may be in better shape than you think."

The knot in his chest loosened a bit. "Thanks. That's nice to hear." He looked over his shoulder at the bench crew. "Time to get back to work."

Twenty minutes later, someone called his name. When he lifted his head, Lucky was on his way over. Now that he thought about it, Lucky hadn't been part of the work crew.

Strange, because the bookstore was closed today. "Hey, Lucky." He laid a plank on the stacked cinderblocks and straightened. "What's up?"

"We're having a meeting about the Apple Grove location and we need your input. Mom asked me to come get you."

"You're meeting now?" Trent pulled off his gloves and fell into step beside Lucky.

"It'll be a short one."

"Who called it?"

"She did."

"You're kidding."

"I told her it could be handled when she gets back from Africa, but she said it was too important to put off."

"Alrighty, then." He took the steps fast but made sure he didn't bump into the decorated arch. Flowers had been added to the greenery.

Lucky headed for the library and Trent followed. The door was open.

"The Wenches are part of this meeting?"

"We figured they might as well be since they were on site anyway."

Trent took off his hat and nodded to the women seated in a large circle, each in a wingback chair that matched her signature color. Dining chairs had been added to the circle. Andy had joined the group, along with Oksana, Lucky's business partner and fiancée.

Lucky took one empty chair and Trent settled into the other one.

Desiree started things off by looking straight at him. "Your brother gave me a heads-up yesterday that he'd accidentally tipped you off about a family secret."

"I'm sure he didn't mean to."

"I'm sure he didn't, either, and it's fine, because he also let me know you're putting a lot of time and effort into finding M.R. Morrison."

The pieces fell into place. "You know where he is, don't you?"

She smiled. "Yes, I do." She left her purple chair, walked over to him and held out her hand.

He got to his feet and took it. "I don't—"

"Allow me to introduce myself. I'm M.R Morrison."

His jaw dropped. "You can't be."

"Ah, but I am. Everyone in this room will back me up. So will the folks outside working on the bench project. Brit doesn't know, and I haven't told your folks yet, but otherwise, everyone else is in on the secret."

"But he's a man."

"That's what you've been led to believe all these years." She squeezed his hand and let go. Then she waggled her fingers in front of his face. "These hands typed all those books. They came from this brain." She pointed to her head. Then she shrugged and returned to her chair. "Or they came out of the ether. Sometimes it feels like ideas just drop out of nowhere."

"I'm stunned."

"I can see that. But we don't have a lot of time, so please take your seat and put your thinking cap on, because we have a major issue to decide, one that involves many opportunities and many risks."

Nobody had asked him to put his thinking cap on since third grade. But if he'd ever needed to put one on, it was now. Questions bounced around in his head begging to be answered, but her brisk attitude told him now was not the time to satisfy his curiosity. Action was required.

"To quickly bring you up to speed, I created the pseudonym because thirty-plus years ago male Western authors sold better. Times have changed. Is it time to uncloak myself?"

Trent opened his mouth to give her a *hell, yes* when she stopped him with a raised hand.

"Think before you answer. It would ensure the Apple Grove store's success. It would bring more business to this shop, too. And to the town. It might help remove any remaining prejudice against women who write Westerns. But it will certainly result in a loss of privacy to this family, to Rowdy Ranch. It could also change the character of this sleepy little town we all love."

He stared at her. "Are you planning to make this decision now? Today, of all days?"

"No, I'm not. But I would like to take a preliminary vote of the people in this room about the advisability of the idea."

"What about the rest of the family?"

"We'll discuss it when I get back from Africa. Before you vote, know that if we do this, we won't be shy about it. We'll go for broke. We can't pull that off for the June grand opening, but maybe by August, we'd be ready to pull out all the stops. I want a show of hands. Who's—"

"I shouldn't vote. I'm not really a member of this—"

"Yes, you are." Desiree held his gaze. "As of this moment, you're family." She shifted her attention to the group. "Okay. Who's in favor of introducing the world to the real M.R. Morrison?"

Thinking he'd be in the minority, he raised his hand. So did everyone else. Even Desiree.

She grinned. "Looks like this is a go for broke crowd, after all."

Trent did a mental fist pump. Hot damn.

40

Something had changed. Brit pinpointed it as the moment Trent had emerged from the house after whatever Lucky had called him inside for. When he'd walked back out, his stride had been subtly different, more energized and purposeful.

During the picnic lunch they'd all eaten while sitting on the benches, he'd seemed more animated. Even with her. Whenever he'd caught her eye, he'd given her a secret smile as if he couldn't wait to tell her something.

On the drive back to his cabin to change clothes, she waited to see if he'd say why he'd been summoned. Finally she couldn't stand it. "It's probably none of my business, but I'm curious about your trip into the house earlier."

"Desiree called a meeting to talk about the new Apple Grove location for L'Amour and More."

"On her wedding day?"

"She wanted to settle a couple of things before she left for Africa." The statement was matter-of-fact, but a current of excitement ran through it.

"Huh. Well, I guess that makes sense. The grand opening's only a few days after she gets back.

I just figured she was leaving the details to you, Lucky and Oksana."

"Which she is. There are just... other considerations."

He was being deliberately vague about something that was clearly a major shift, which made her more curious. But continuing to pester him for details would be obnoxious since it really was none of her business.

Maybe he was excited about the grand opening. The *Sentinel* had run a story on it recently and her mom had suggested making a day trip of going up to check it out. "Will you be up there that weekend?"

"Yes, ma'am." He glanced at her. "Want to go?"

Her breath caught. "I—"

"Just an idea. You don't have to decide yet."

"Okay."

He pulled into the parking space at the end of the flagstone walk. "You can have first shower."

"Thanks. I want to wash my hair, so I'll need time to dry it." As soon as he shut off the motor, she opened her door and climbed out.

"I don't think you need to rush, though. We have a couple of hours."

She was well aware of it. Before he'd proclaimed his love, she'd expected they'd spend some quality time in bed before the ceremony. Was he still thinking that way?

He caught up with her as she headed for the house. "I have a request."

Her traitorous body reacted. If he wanted to make love, would she have the willpower to turn him down? "What's that?"

"Sit on the swing with me for a few minutes before you go in."

Odd, very odd. Maybe now he'd tell her about the meeting. "Okay." She climbed the steps and held the armrest of the swing to steady it as she sat down.

He settled next to her, his thigh touching hers. Then he slid his arm around her shoulders.

The warmth of his body set her on fire as it always had. She swallowed. "Do you want to make out? Is that what's going on?"

"No. I want to lay all my cards on the table."

"I thought you did that yesterday." Her heart started playing the bongos.

"I laid down some of them, but it seems I had some up my sleeve, cards I didn't realize were there."

"Like what?"

"Dallas was right about the swing. I was coming out of my funk when I bought it. I was ready to start living again, create a new dream."

She began to shake. "Trent, don't—"

"And then there you were, wanting a baby, so of course I said yes, because I wanted the baby. And I wanted you. I just didn't understand that yet."

This couldn't be happening. She squeezed her eyes shut as fear washed over her. "You're going to propose, aren't you?"

"Yes, I am." He shifted on the swing. "Will you look at me while I do it? Please?"

She opened her eyes and turned her head, scared to death but needing to confirm the bad news. Yep. The poor guy really did love her. And some turn of events was driving him to break his promise. "What happened in that meeting?"

"I saw a vision of the future. My future. And I want you to be part of it. You'll want that, too, if you'll just give yourself a chance. I love you, and arrogant ass that I am, I think you love me back. Will you marry me?"

She could barely breathe. "No, Trent. I told you not to do this. You promised you wouldn't."

"Because I didn't understand then. I'm breaking that promise because it's holding us back from something amazing."

"What vision? Are they putting you in charge of the Apple Grove store?"

"No."

"Then what's all this stuff about the future?"

"Our future. Yours, mine and Montana's. I want us to be a family, living together, loving each other, giving Montana a brother or sister. I want it all, Brittany."

"Well I don't." She pushed away from him and stood, hoping her legs would hold her. "Sorry, Trent. You've got the wrong girl."

"No, I've got the right girl because you picked me. You picked me! There's a voice inside of you saying I'm the one, which is why I'm the father of your child. Listen to that voice!"

His words hit home. She had picked him. She'd engineered this whole mess and now that foolish man wanted to marry her. She couldn't let him make that mistake. "I'm taking a shower." She ran into the house, stripped off her clothes in the bathroom and turned on the water.

Then she stood under it and cried, cried for the little girl who hadn't been enough to make her daddy stay, the big girl who'd set ridiculous standards for the man she'd deign to marry because if she took that plunge, she might discover that she was the one who was lacking.

Trent was everything she'd ever wanted, but she didn't dare test whether she was everything he'd ever wanted. Oh, but she'd tied him to her for life, hadn't she? Tied him to her, but guaranteed he'd never really get to know her because they'd live separately.

Eventually the water turned cold and she got out. Once she was dressed, she took her makeup, her small mirror and the hairdryer into the kitchen. An ice cube from the fridge reduced the puffiness under her eyes from her crying jag.

Tossing it in the sink, she went to the front door and stuck her head out. He was still on the swing, staring at the mountains. "The bathroom's all yours, but I used all the hot water, so you might want to wait a bit before showering."

"Nope." He stood. "A cold shower sounds like just what I need."

"If you say so." She opened the door wide and started back toward the kitchen.

He followed her in there and took her by the shoulders.

The warmth of his hands and his gentle massage brought a lump to her throat. "Trent." She would not fling herself into his arms. For his sake as well as hers.

"Brittany." He perfectly matched her tone.

"Are you going to keep bugging me?"

"Yes. At least until you can tell me with a straight face that you don't love me."

"I don't love you."

"Say it while you're looking at me." He slowly turned her around.

She lifted her head and met the warm, compassionate glow in his eyes. He was so beautiful. She'd have to lie through her teeth. "I don't—

"Save your breath. Any fool can tell you're nuts about me."

She couldn't make herself deny it. Especially when he was in this crazy mood. He was way too appealing. "What's gotten into you?"

"Like I said, I see the whole picture, now. We were supposed to meet on the eve of your birthday, when we were both ready to change our lives. Montana was meant to be. You and I are destined to spend a lifetime together." He sighed. "And you don't believe a word I'm saying."

"Nope."

"You will."

"Did they serve gummies at that meeting?"

He laughed. "No." Then he dipped his head and gave her a quick kiss. "If you want me, I'll be in the shower."

She stood there in shock, his kiss making her lips tingle, his words urging her to run after him. But she didn't have his confidence in the future.

Or in herself.

41

Trent was flying on instruments, trusting that even though he couldn't see what was going on in Brittany's head, eventually her heart would take the controls and they'd land safely.

He didn't know that for sure, but how could this turn out any other way? They hadn't served gummies at the meeting but he'd come out with a whole new perspective on his life. He was officially part of this incredible family and its exciting future. Brittany should be, too.

He shaved before showering to give the water time to warm up. It wasn't icy when he got in but it wasn't warm, either. He didn't linger.

But she shouldn't have been able to use up the hot water, even with washing her hair. Cheyenne hadn't cut corners on anything in this cabin, including the hot water tank.

One conclusion troubled him — that she'd stood in the shower crying until the water turned cold. Living with sisters had taught him that a woman who wanted to hide her tears might use the shower to disguise them. Guys would just go pound on something and pretend the tears were sweat.

By the time he finished dressing and came out of the bedroom, she was ready to go. And wearing her silverbelly, which went great with her sparkly jeans and denim jacket. "You look terrific."

"Thank you." Her voice softened. "You, too."

"Thank you." He'd take any crumb while he waited for her to offer the whole cake. "I was afraid you wouldn't wear the hat since you're kind of mad at me."

"That would be cutting off my nose to spite my face. This is the most beautiful hat I've ever seen and I plan to wear it every chance I get, except when it might get dirty."

"I'm glad you like it. I was meant to buy it for you. That's why you never got it for yourself. It was supposed to be a present from me."

"If you say so." She picked up her phone. "Ready?"

"Let's do it." He ushered her out to the porch.

"I never asked how they're planning to feed all those people."

He paused before closing the door. "Uh-oh."

"What?"

"Potluck."

"Oh, geez. It was on the invitation. *No gifts, but please bring a dish to share.* I didn't shop for a gift but then I forgot all about the dish."

"It's been a busy week."

"Really? I didn't notice."

"Let me see what's in the cupboard." He headed back into the cabin.

She walked in right behind him. "You can't just take a bag of chips. This is a wedding."

"A super casual one. We'll be eating on those benches, so chips are way better than some sloppy casserole you'll spill all over yourself." He reached up and pulled down two bags. "Take your pick — tortilla or potato."

"Tortilla." She took the bag and held out her other hand. "But give me both. You're driving."

"That I am, and we'd better get a move on."

She looked at her phone as she hurried out the door. "Yeah, it's later than I thought. Weren't they going to block off the road about now and direct the people from town to the overflow lot?"

"We should just make it before they do that." He helped her into the truck, jogged to the driver's side and climbed behind the wheel. Once he had the engine running, he tapped the button for the radio.

"Are you trying to soften me up?"

"Yes, ma'am." He grimaced as Deana Carter belted out *Did I Shave My Legs for This.* "But never mind." He turned it off. Not the picture he wanted her to have of married life.

"For the record, I'm not worried you'd turn into a beer-drinking, TV-watching slob of a husband."

"But you might be worried I'd leave." He held his breath. Saying that could be a huge mistake.

She was quiet for a couple seconds. Seemed like an eternity. "You've been talking to Ella. Or Marsh."

"Marsh." He hesitated. "Also for the record, I can't imagine leaving you."

"Could you imagine leaving Cheryl when you married her?"

"No, but she—"

"Cheated, lied, was mean to you."

"Yes."

"I wouldn't do those things, but I could do other things that would get on your nerves."

"And I guarantee I'll do things that would get on yours. I'm not perfect."

"Yeah, you are, except for your sudden and annoying fixation on love and marriage."

"I've got plenty of flaws. Like everybody does. But I'll do my best to make you happy and all I ask is that you give back the love I give to you. I know you're good at that, Casey Cougar."

"What the heck has Casey got to do with us?"

"Rance told me you hold a special place in the hearts of Wagon Train folks. They loved you as Casey and you loved them back, game after game through your entire high school career. I wish I'd been there to see it."

She went quiet again, for longer this time. "But it wasn't me," she said, her voice almost a whisper. "I was someone else."

"Oh, but it was you twirling on that barstool. It was you making love to me. It was you singing *Brown Eyed Girl.* It's no wonder you were the best Casey they ever had because your spirit was shining through that costume. If there's a video out there I want to see it, but even if there isn't I have no trouble picturing you as—"

"You just missed the turnoff." Her voice sounded funny, like her throat was clogged.

He pulled over so he could make a U-turn, but first he needed to find out what was going on with her. "Brittany?"

She kept her face toward the window. "Just turn around and go back. They'll put up that barricade any minute."

"Are you crying?"

"Just turn around and go back!"

She was crying. He was sure of it. And she had no purse, no tissues. Dallas had started carrying a bandana, but he hadn't picked up that habit yet. He opened the console, found a napkin from a Buffalo takeout meal and handed it over her shoulder. "Here."

"Thanks. Now drive, please."

He did, and the short delay had cost them. There was a line reaching back down the road and he was coming in from the other direction. Evidently he'd been just a little ahead of that caravan, but he'd been so focused on winning her over he hadn't noticed.

Now he had to wait for a kind soul to let him in. Because it was Wagon Train, someone did. But he was stuck in a slow-moving line. Down the road, before the curve, stood the barricade. "We'll have to park in the overflow."

"I know."

He glanced at her. "How're you doing?"

"Let's see." Dragging in a breath, she pulled down the visor and flipped up the cover on the mirror. "I look like I've been crying." She crumpled up the napkin in her fist. "Got ice?"

"Fresh out."

"Since we'll need to walk for a couple of minutes, I'll look better by the time we get there."

"I'm sorry. I shouldn't have said—"

"Don't apologize for saying nice things." She took another ragged breath as she stared out the windshield. "You were right about what you said when we were on the swing. I picked you, so this is all on me."

"Thank God you picked me, and it's not all on you. Not anymore. That's my point. It's on us and we—"

"My plan to live separately while we raise Montana was designed to keep you from discovering I'm not as great as you think I am."

His heart stalled. There it was. A big scary stumbling block of fear. "I've only seen the tip of the iceberg. I'm convinced you're ten times greater."

"And that's what scares me! You think I can live up to that?"

"Yes."

"Well, that makes one of us."

_42_

Speaking the truth made Brit feel lighter, a lot lighter. She'd admitted to Ella that Trent's declaration of love terrified her. Now he knew her real motivation for living apart. Since she'd bound them together for life, he needed to understand she was a big fat coward.

As Trent backed into a parking spot, she checked her puffy eyes again in the visor mirror. She'd been blessed with dark lashes and didn't use mascara, which saved her from looking like a raccoon on the few times she got weepy.

The puffiness was mostly gone and her hat would shade her red eyes. That was helpful because she'd just figured out her mom and Doc Bradbury would also park in the overflow lot.

Trent opened her door. "I'll take the chips." He tucked them in one arm and helped her down.

"We need to look for Doc Bradbury's white SUV."

"I see several."

"Look for a license plate that says PRLYWHT."

"Then you're in luck. They just pulled in."

"Good. We can walk down there with them and won't have to hunt through the crowd to find them."

"If you'll go over so they'll know we're here, I'll text my folks and see if they can save us two more seats. They only planned on saving two."

"And I thought we'd be there in time to save two more."

"My fault."

She gazed at him, warmth filling her chest. "We screwed it up together. It'll work out." Waving her arms in the air, she hurried toward the SUV.

Her mom and Elaine came toward her holding Tupperware containers.

"Love the hat." Her mom's gaze swept over her. "Where's your purse?"

"Decided I didn't need one."

"What about tissues? You're going to a wedding, and—"

"Good point." It wasn't the wedding she needed them for.

"Take some." Her mom handed her a couple.

She tucked them in her pocket. "I see you guys remembered to make a dish. We forgot and had to bring chips."

Her mom grinned. "Don't admit it. Just say it was the most practical choice."

"You sound like Trent. He's texting his folks to save four seats near the front."

"That's great," Elaine said, "but why are you in the overflow? I thought you'd already be down there."

Her mom gave the doc a nudge.

"Never mind." Her eyes twinkled. "Priorities."

Brit flushed. "That's not why. Let's go get Trent and start down."

"I'm right here." He came up beside her, the chips still tucked against his chest. He shoved his phone in his pocket and tipped his hat. "Nice to see you again, Margaret. And you must be Doc Bradbury."

"Elaine." She balanced the Tupperware and shook his hand. "I've had the pleasure of having your brother in my chair."

"I promise to make an appointment. I've been meaning to, but—"

"No pressure." She smiled. "Folks always get apologetic around me, like I'm evaluating their teeth for signs of neglect."

"You don't?"

"Oh, I do, but I'd never say anything. Yours are beautiful, by the way."

He blushed. "Thank you. Hey, I hear the band starting up, so we'd better take off. My folks did save four seats, but we don't want to get in at the last minute."

"You two lead the way," her mom said. "You know the layout."

'Yes, ma'am." Trent reached for Brit's hand, slid his fingers through hers and started off, his stride shorter than usual.

She hadn't noticed that before. Those long legs could cover more ground, but he adjusted his pace when they walked together. "I can take one of those chips."

"I've got 'em." He squeezed her hand.

She squeezed back. Was he dreading this wedding? Maybe not anymore, but she couldn't ask since they weren't alone. The music grew louder as they approached the curve in the road.

"Hey, Brit, have you seen Nick Reynolds?"

She glanced over her shoulder at her mother. "Who?"

"Nick Reynolds. Cheyenne and Clint's dad. The actor. He's supposed to be here."

"Haven't seen him."

"How about Derek Sanders, Bret and Gil's dad? I heard he was coming, too. I might not recognize him but I'd sure recognize Nick."

"I've got nuthin', Mom. Sorry." She looked over at Trent. "Have you heard anything about random dads showing up for the wedding?"

"No, ma'am. But since we're on the subject, do you know anything about Rance's dad? He's never said a word about him, which makes me afraid to ask."

Her mom snorted. "Don't bother. I feel sorry for Rance. He drew the short straw."

"What do you mean?"

"His dad's Irving Quick. He writes thrillers, so I started reading them. They weren't bad, but I'll never read another one."

"Why not?"

"After several years, when he hadn't returned as far as I knew, I researched him online and found an interview where he raved about his wife and two kids. No mention of Rance."

"Ouch."

"Yeah. You know Rance has looked him up, too. Has to hurt."

"That's a shame." Brit glanced at Trent. "But at least you know not to bring it up."

"Yep. Thanks, Margaret."

Nobody tried to talk after that because the curve was dead ahead and the bandstand wasn't far from it. House Wine was playing a sweet country tune with no lyrics, but they had the volume turned up so the music would reach all the way to the house.

When Brit walked around the curve, she sucked in a breath. She'd watched the venue take shape, but now, with the band playing and the benches nearly filled, the importance of the event finally registered. "Wow."

Behind her, Elaine gasped, too. "Oh, my. It looks like a movie set complete with all the extras."

Cecily hurried toward them, followed by two other servers from the Buffalo who divested them of the Tupperware and the chips. A large tent across from the bandstand and dance floor had been turned into a kitchen, complete with two refrigerators and a stovetop.

Cecily flashed Trent a teasing grin and raised her voice to be heard over the band. "Chips? Really?"

He laughed. "Uh-huh. Put you to work, did they?"

"I volunteered. Desiree's one of my all-time favorite customers. Go grab your seats, guys. We're close to kickoff."

Trent scanned the crowd. "I see my folks. This way." He led them down the left side aisle.

His folks sat on the end of the front bench. Two broad-shouldered men in Western jackets perched on the end closest to the center aisle, leaving the middle open with four paper plates held down with rocks.

Brit smiled. "Who do you suppose came up with the plate and rock routine?"

"My mom. She'd do that at Little League games for my grandparents."

"Whoa, front row seats." Elaine chuckled. "It's nice to have connections."

"Hang on." Brit's mom grabbed Trent's arm before he'd reached his parents.

He stopped and glanced back at her. "Problem?"

"No, I just want to be sure. Yep. The guy next to the guy on the end is Nick. The other one is probably Derek. I just wanted to make sure before I say hello."

Brit blinked. "You know them?"

"Not Derek, but Nick used to come in to get his teeth cleaned."

"Oh. Okay." The sparkle of anticipation in her mother's eyes startled her. If she didn't know better, she'd say her mom had a crush on Nick Reynolds.

When Trent made their presence known, Trent's dad stood and Brit quickly introduced her mom and Elaine to the Armstrongs. After some discussion about who should sit where, Harry and Vanessa moved to the middle of the group. Brit's mom and Elaine took the right side with her mom next to Vanessa.

Brit ended up sandwiched between Harry and Trent. Good thing they were in the front row or she wouldn't have been able to see a thing. She searched for a neutral topic to discuss with Harry. "So, Harry, how's the weather back home?"

He gave her a smile. "Terrible. Late snow storm. Good thing they got it instead of us, huh?"

"Sure is. We lucked out." And she was out of topics.

"I hear you were the high school mascot."

Again with the mascot? She looked at Trent.

"I didn't tell him. Must have been one of the McLintocks."

"Desiree. Naturally she was at all the games. Her kids were in everything. Impressive bunch."

"Absolutely."

"She has some footage of you in the cougar suit, but we didn't have time to look at it. She said your mom likely has even more. They used to sit together at the games."

"Footage." Trent gave her arm a nudge. "That's what I'm talking about. Movie night. All we need is the popcorn."

She made a face and he laughed. Was he doing okay? Sure seemed like it. But if the ceremony got to him, she was there to help him through it.

Right. She was likely the person who'd require support. With her emotions veering from despair to laughter at the drop of a hat, she cherished the firm grip of his hand and the solid bulk of him next to her.

He knew the truth about her now, and he hadn't pulled away in disgust. If anything, he'd doubled down. Was he really, truly in love with her? Slowly, cautiously, she mentally peeked through her spread fingers at the vision he'd laid out.

She didn't believe in it yet. But oh, how she wanted to.

_**43**_

Three months ago when Desiree and Andy had announced they'd settled on a date for their wedding, everyone partying at the Buffalo had cheered. Everyone except Trent. He'd dreaded this moment.

The minister set a mic stand on the top step. Turned on the mic, blew in it, turned it off. Then he took his place on the porch.

Brittany's anxiety traveled through her fingers, making him highly aware of her agitation. He sent back all the love he could through their clasped hands.

He no longer dreaded what was to come. He needed this wedding, maybe as much as Desiree and Andy did. It was the final test of whether he'd healed the damage Cheryl had done. And a chance for Brittany to see a different future than the one she was still clinging to.

The band ended their final instrumental tune and the guests grew quiet. When the opening chords of _Bless the Broken Road_ by Rascal Flatts filled the air, he tensed, anticipation rolling through him.

Rance had played it on a boom box for the rehearsal. It hadn't been very loud. The lyrics had been indistinct, the impact minimal. Trent had heard it many times in the past. After his marriage had broken up, he'd dismissed the song's message as hogwash.

Not anymore. The band's vibrant, full-throated rendition of two people finding each other after years of love's disappointments swept through him, engulfing him in a wave of emotion. It was a perfect song for Desiree and Andy. And for him. And Brittany, if she'd let him into her heart.

Hand in hand, Buck and Marybeth nodded to the guests as they strolled down the carpeted middle aisle dressed in their good jeans, boots, shirts and hats. No fancy dresses or rented outfits. At the end of the aisle they separated, Buck going right to stand beside the steps and Marybeth turning left to take a position on the other side.

Sky and Penny followed, clearly bursting with eagerness, barely managing to stay in time with the music. Beau and Jess also looked like they were ready to get this show on the road. Clint flashed his typical jaunty grin as he and Tyra made the long walk down the carpeted aisle.

The birth order parade continued with Cheyenne and Kendall, Cheyenne's eyes shining and Kendall looking happy enough to float if Cheyenne let go of her. Marsh and Ella had the proud walk of two parents-to-be.

Bret and Molly's pace was more measured, their fingers laced together, their gaze steady. Gil and Faye shimmered with energy and added a subtle dance step as they moved down the aisle.

The excitement sparkling in Lucky and Oksana's eyes was likely because their love was so new. But after that meeting, Trent read more into their confident stride.

Behind them, Rance walked backward as he pulled a red wagon and talked softly to the five little kids tucked into it. Angie and Dallas followed closely, reaching out every so often to steady one of the toddlers. Dallas glanced quickly over at Trent as if checking on him, too.

Trent acknowledged the look with a nod and got a relieved smile in return.

At the end of the aisle, Rance wheeled the wagon to the right. Then each dad stepped forward to take charge of his child. Sky took Susie and Cheyenne picked up Jodie with no problem, but when Beau reached for Mav, she clung to her best buddy Zach and wouldn't budge.

"So cute," Brittany murmured.

Trent's dad chuckled. "I remember those days."

And Trent wanted those days. With Brittany by his side. He glanced at her. "We need a wagon."

She met his gaze. "Yes, we do."

He liked what he saw in her eyes. It looked like the beginning of hope.

"They're leaving those two in the wagon and just taking Zach's little sister," Trent's mom said. "They may live to regret that."

The music ended and House Wine allowed silence to settle over the gathering once again. Then their keyboardist played the opening notes of Aloe Blacc and Lee Ann Rimes' rendition of *I Do.*

Trent smiled. That song, about resistance to commitment, a resistance that finally dissolved, had to be Desiree's choice, her gift to Andy. And it sure fit his and Brittany's situation.

Everyone stood and turned toward the back of the venue. Trent let go of Brittany's hand so they could do the same. Bracing herself on his shoulder, she rose to her toes.

He slipped a steadying arm around her waist and leaned down. "Can you see?"

She nodded. "Well enough.

He tightened his grip on her waist. Height had its advantages. With most of the town's tallest residents in the wedding party, he had a decent view of Desiree and Andy as they walked down the aisle hand-in-hand.

Nobody was giving that lady away.

She hadn't dressed up, either. Not much, anyway. Her purple Western shirt might be new. He'd never seen the purple boots before, either. She'd added a purple feather to her hat, but it was a hat he'd seen her wear many times.

Andy looked like he'd just been crowned king of the world. Desiree's steady gaze remained on the altar at the end of the aisle, but Andy kept sneaking glances at his bride, as if he still couldn't quite believe his good fortune.

Trent almost missed Brittany's soft swallow. Glancing down, his heart turned over. Tears shimmered in her eyes, but she didn't look sad. Her face glowed with happiness. Was that for Desiree and Andy? Or did it have something to do with him?

As Desiree and Andy drew closer, Zach and Mav climbed out of the wagon. Beau reached for Mav but she was off like a shot. Bret had his hands full with Zach's baby sister. The kids made a beeline for their beloved Granny Dez and Grandpa Andy.

Desiree and Andy reacted as if they'd anticipated it. Crouching down in sync, they held out their arms. Desiree picked up Mav and Andy lifted Zach. Then they continued down the aisle toward the minister as if it was all part of the show.

Between the tender song and the sight of Desiree and Andy carrying their grandchildren with them to the altar, the crowd morphed into a sniffing, throat-clearing group. Trent's dad cleared his. Then Trent had to do the same.

Mopping her tear-streaked cheeks with a tissue, Brittany turned to him.

Where had that tissue come from?

She lifted her head, her blue eyes luminous. "I get it. Trent." Her voice shook. "I *get* it. I want... I want all this. And I love—" She choked up. "I love you."

He forgot about the tissue. Forgot that a wedding was in progress. She was looking at him the way Andy had looked at Desiree. He tried to speak. The words stuck in his throat.

She gripped the front of his shirt in both hands. "If the offer still stands, my answer is *yes.*"

He groaned and gathered her close, his heart beating so hard and fast he was afraid he'd pass out.

"Son." His dad laid a gentle hand on his shoulder. "Time to sit. It's starting."

He kept hold of her as they both eased down to the bench, hip to hip, his arm around her shoulders, her hand on his knee. He put his lips close to her ear. "You're sure?"

She nodded vigorously, her hair tickling his cheek.

"I love you."

She tilted her head and looked up at him, her lips moving in a silent *I love you, too.*

He wanted to shout for joy. He wanted to kiss her and then kiss her some more.

"We need to listen to this," she murmured, squeezing his knee. "It's important."

Tucking her in close, he turned his attention to Desiree and Andy, who'd apparently chosen to take their vows while they each held a grandchild. They stood facing each other one step below the mic.

The minister welcomed everyone with the usual opening words. Then he turned the ceremony over to the bride and groom.

Desiree said something softly to the toddler in her arms. Mav nestled her head against her grandmother's shoulder and sucked on her thumb.

Taking a deep breath, Desiree focused on Andy. "I never thought I'd be standing at the altar, but I never expected to fall in love with a man who wouldn't take no for an answer. You're as stubborn as a mule, Andy. And I love you for it. So here I am, and I hope you know what you're doing because you're never getting rid of me." She swallowed. "I'm all in, my love."

Trent looked at Brittany, who'd clearly soaked up every word. She didn't move a muscle as Andy prepared to say his piece.

First he repositioned Zach, who stared out at the crowd in obvious fascination.

Andy cleared his throat and began. "You're a challenge, Dez, and I didn't think I needed one at this stage of my life. Seems I did." His voice grew husky. "I need you more than I need to breathe." He cleared his throat again. "But I intend to keep on breathing, so you'll have to put up with me for a long time. But no matter how many days or years I'm given, they'll never be enough to show you how much I love you. You're worth the wait, Granny Dez."

The minister completed the ceremony, getting a firm *I do* from both bride and groom. With Buck and Marybeth's help, rings were exchanged despite the grandchildren in their arms, and after the minister pronounced them husband and wife, they even managed a brief kiss.

Trent and Brittany rose to their feet along with the rest of the crowd, clapping and cheering as the band launched into George Strait's *Here for a Good Time.*

Desiree turned toward the mic. "We're skipping the recessional folks! Everybody follow Andy and me. These kids are hungry. Let's eat!"

Trent laid a hand on Brittany's shoulder. "Let's go find a quiet spot and—"

"But first don't we need to tell our folks?"

"Absolutely tell us." Trent's dad turned toward them. "Because if I'm not mistaken, you two just got engaged."

"They *what*?" His mom spun toward them.

Margaret did a double-take, too. "Did I hear the word *engaged*?"

"You did, Mom." Brittany's voice trembled. "Trent asked me and I've accepted."

Her mom's whoop of joy and Brittany's watery smile were all Trent needed to fall in with the plan. His dad clapped him on the back and his mom gave him a hug. Then she gathered Brittany into a tight embrace as her mother let go of her.

Margaret's enthusiastic hug came next, and then even Doc Bradbury joined in the hug fest. Trent got up close and personal with everyone except the woman he loved. A conversation about heading down to the feast so they could celebrate made him wonder how many hours he'd have to wait before he kissed her.

Then she took control of the situation. "You all go ahead. Trent and I will be along later. We have some stuff to discuss."

Yes.

"Can I bring up just one thing before we part ways?" Margaret glanced at her daughter. "It's about tomorrow."

"This doesn't have to change anything, Mom. We'll still do our Mother's Day like we planned." She looked at him. "Right?"

He bit back his disappointment. "Well, sure. I mean, if you have a tradition, then—"

"We do." Margaret's cheeks turned pink. "But under the circumstances, if it's okay with you and your folks, and Desiree doesn't mind, it seems like it would be nice for Brit and me to celebrate at the ranch. That's only if it works for everyone."

"I'm sure it would," Vanessa said. "Desiree will be thrilled about this engagement, too. If you come for the day, you could also reconnect with Nick. It seemed like he'd enjoy spending time with you."

Margaret's flush deepened. "Well, only if it suits everyone. Anyway, Brit, go have your private moment with Trent. I'll check with Desiree and let you know."

"Thanks, Mom. It sounds like a great plan." Brittany looked like she was trying not to laugh.

Trent waited until they were out of earshot. "Does she have a thing for this Nick character?"

"I think so."

"What do we know about him? Other than the fact he didn't want to stick around and be a dad. We should ask Desiree what she thinks about—"

"Are you watching out for my mother?" Amusement sparkled in her eyes.

"Yes, I am. She's been hurt before, and—"

"I think she can take care of herself. I'm happy that she's shown an interest in someone. If Desiree lets him stay at the house, he can't be all bad."

"Maybe not, but I still want to do some research on the guy."

"Later, right?"

"Definitely later."

"Where's a good place for us to make out — I mean *talk*."

"We're on a ranch. I've heard behind the barn is a prime spot."

"Then let's go."

"Yes, ma'am." He took her hand and they started toward the large red structure Gigabyte called home. "In the barn might be even better. You could meet my horse."

"I probably should. What if he doesn't approve of me?"

"He will. I told him about you when I was trying to decide about the baby. He thought I should go for it. He's a gelding, so I'm not surprised he'd say that."

"A talking horse? Now I really want to meet him."

"He doesn't do it for everybody."

"Just you?"

"Pretty much."

"What's he look like?"

"He's a bay. Dark coat, black stockings, a white star on his forehead. And before we go in there, I'm only planning to kiss you. No funny business. The entire town's on the property. No telling who could accidentally wander in."

"Will there be funny business when we get back to your cabin?"

"Count on it." That revved his engines. "How soon do you think we can leave?"

"Not too soon. This is a special time. A special wedding. It pulled me out of my dark place. It gave me you. I have people to thank. We have an engagement to announce."

"Then we'll stay as long as you want. So what was the gamechanger? When Desiree and Andy picked up the kids?"

"That was what put me over the top, realizing that someday we might be grandparents.

I want to be that kind of grandparent, and you'll be a great granddad."

"Don't rush it." Sliding back the bar that secured the barn door, he opened it just enough for them to slip through.

She laughed as she walked in. "Well, you will be. Where's Gigabyte?"

"First stall on the left, munching on his dinner." He kept the door open to let in shafts of light from the setting sun. "Hey, buddy, I brought someone to see you. This is the woman I'm going to marry."

Her breath hitched. "That gives me goosebumps."

"Good or bad ones?"

"Good ones. Very good ones. Hey, there, Gigabyte. Gonna leave that hay net for a minute and come over and see me?"

The big bay obligingly abandoned his food and walked toward the stall door so she could rub his neck and scratch his nose.

Trent stood back, watching her make friends with his horse while dreams and schemes filled his head and his heart — they'd get a horse for her, take long rides on the weekend, cuddle in his bed after the sun went down, make love....

"You're a handsome guy, Gigabyte," she murmured. "Just like your rider."

"I heard that." He started toward her.

"You were supposed to."

"Flattery will get you kissed."

"I heard kissing was part of the plan for sneaking out to the barn." She turned away from the stall.

"Then we should get started." He tugged her warm body close, hungry for her touch. "I love you. I love you so much."

She wound her arms around his neck. "Clearly you must or you wouldn't have put up with my nonsense. I gave you so much grief and I'm so sorry."

"You didn't give me grief." He tightened his hold, his blood heating. "You gave me a challenge."

"You stole that line from Andy."

"I'll probably steal more. And get tips. You and Desiree have a lot in common."

"Good thing you're stubborn like Andy, then."

"Good thing you love that about me."

"I love everything about you, especially that. It's why we're here, about to share our first kiss after getting engaged, hint, hint."

"Yes, ma'am. Coming right up." He nudged back her hat. "Close your eyes, Gigabyte." Then he claimed her mouth. And nearly lost his cool. He hadn't kissed her like this for days, had wondered if he'd ever kiss her like this again.

Struggling with emotions stronger than he was prepared for, he lifted his head. "I missed you." He swallowed. "I was afraid I'd lost you."

"But you didn't." She looked up at him, her gaze warm, her voice husky. "And now I'm yours forever."

"That's not nearly long enough." He settled in, his fears calmed, his heart expanding and his forgotten dreams within reach. All because the woman in his arms had left her purse.

New York Times bestselling author Vicki Lewis Thompson's love affair with cowboys started with the Lone Ranger, continued through Maverick, and took a turn south of the border with Zorro. She views cowboys as the Western version of knights in shining armor, rugged men who value honor, honesty and hard work. Fortunately for her, she lives in the Arizona desert, where broad-shouldered, lean-hipped cowboys abound. Blessed with such an abundance of inspiration, she only hopes that she can do them justice.

For more information about this prolific author, visit her website and sign up for her newsletter. She loves connecting with readers.

VickiLewisThompson.com

9 781638 039211